Rainbow Eyes

ISBN: 0-9842638-0-2
ISBN-13: 9780984263806

www.Chakramid.com

Rainbow Eyes

Chakramid Reflections

Mary Jo Shaffer

TABLE OF CONTENTS

Foreword
Introduction

First Power Pack   1
Accepting an Invitation   3
1st Chakra – "I have"   7
2nd Chakra – "I feel"   19
3rd Chakra – "I act"   31
4th Chakra – "I love"   43

Second Power Pack   57
5th Chakra – "I speak"   59
6th Chakra – "I see"   73
7th Chakra – "I know"   85
At the End, a New Beginning   97

Appendices   101
Appendix A – 1st Chakra   103
Appendix B – 2nd Chakra   105
Appendix C – 3rd Chakra   107
Appendix D – 4th Chakra   109
Appendix E – 5th Chakra   111
Appendix F – 6th Chakra   113
Appendix G – 7th Chakra   115

BONUS SECTION: Journal With Jessica   117
My 1st Chakra Reflections   119
My 2nd Chakra Reflections   121
My 3rd Chakra Reflections   123
My 4th Chakra Reflections   125
My 5th Chakra Reflections   127
My 6th Chakra Reflections   129
My 7th Chakra Reflections   131

FOREWORD

There is no right or wrong way to read this book. You can skip the Introduction if you wish and go right to the story. However, when you are done reading it, you may want to come back to the Introduction if you would like more clarification on Chakras and the Chakramid.

As you read the story, it might be helpful to refer to the corresponding Appendix in the back of the book for each Chakra's overview. Or you may prefer to read the story first and then re-read it after going through the Appendices.

No matter how you read it, enjoy the journey and may it stimulate your own Chakra energy awakening!

INTRODUCTION

What is a Chakra?

"Chakra" is a Sanskrit word (an ancient Eastern Indian language) meaning "wheel" or "circle." According to the principles of Quantum Physics, everything is made up of energy and information, and that is an excellent way to describe your Chakras. Picture your Chakras as seven spinning disks stacked up and evenly spaced along your spinal cord, from the base of your spine to the top of your head. While they are not part of your physical body—you cannot see or feel them—your Chakras do have an enormous effect on your nervous and endocrine systems, as well as on other processes in your body.

Each disk reflects a different color and each is packed full of a specific or focused type of resonating energy, the information that makes up that energy, and what it takes to maintain or balance it. The clockwise rotation action of all of the Chakras in this stack, or energy pathway, helps to distribute energy throughout your entire body. This is accomplished by way of your nervous and circulatory systems so that all of your organs, tissues, and cells receive and benefit from each Chakra's energy vibrations. Chakras also serve to dispose of unwanted or undesirable energy in your body.

Balanced Chakras create a free-flowing subtle-energy network in your body that promotes physical and mental health, vitality, and harmony, as well as spiritual and psychic awareness and evolution. Chakras also play an important role in the prevention or avoidance of illness or disease. Balanced Chakras will create these corresponding results:

1st—A sense of being grounded or connected to the physical

2nd—The ability to feel your emotions and to use them as the guiding sensors they were meant to be

3rd—A profound sense of personal power that propels you forward in all of your endeavors

4th—The joy of experiencing true, unconditional love by using the twin powers of love and forgiveness

5th—The capability to effectively communicate, and to hear and speak your truth

6th—The art of reasoning and unlimited access to imagination and intuitive insight

7th—The profound wisdom that comes from being plugged into your Source and connected to the Universe

Sounds like a perfect system, doesn't it? And it is, but when one or more of the Chakras are out of alignment (causing the spinning action to be counterclockwise, erratic, sluggish, or shut down completely), that Chakra is adversely affected; and consequently, your physical, mental, and spiritual vitality levels suffer.

What is the Chakramid?

The traditional view or representation of the Chakras is a standing or sitting human form studded with seven circles in a rainbow of colors lined up through its middle. It is a very effective way to graphically depict the seven major energy centers in our bodies, but let's consider looking at Chakras in a new, expanded way.

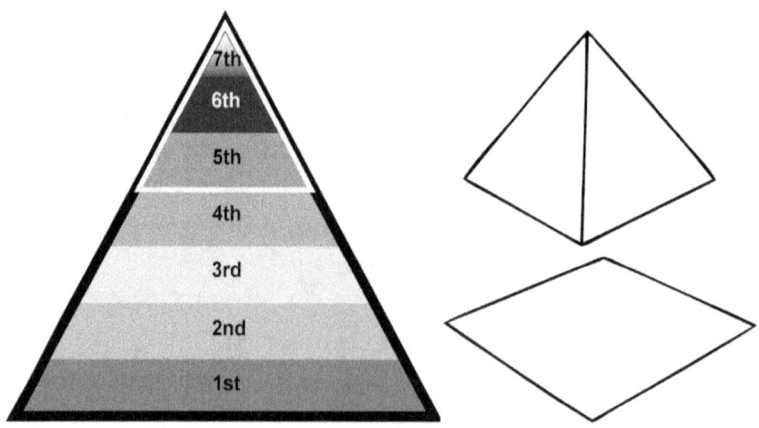

While a pyramid suggests mysticism and mystery, the Chakramid, (or Chakra Pyramid) offers understanding and clarity. The form itself is steeped in Ancient history, but the components of it—a square and four triangles— are simple, contemporary shapes.

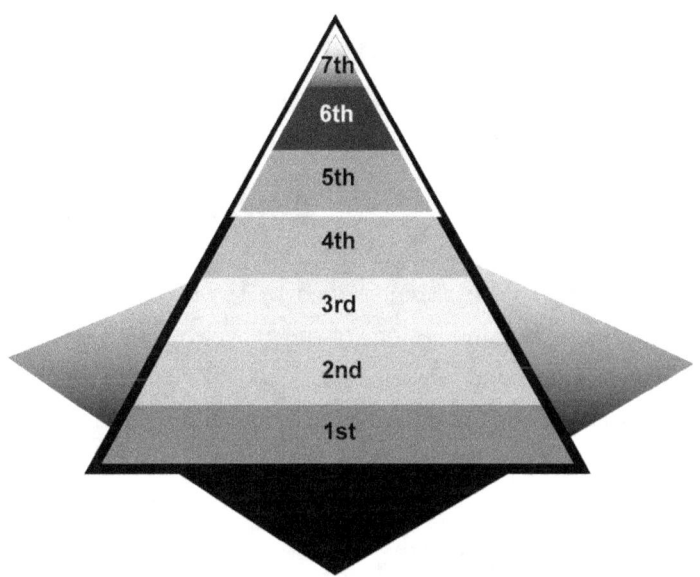

The "form" aspect of the Chakramid shows the Chakras in a definite structure. The Chakramid's cubed base is planted solidly and squarely on the ground and its steep slopes ascend upward to a point or pinnacle. It is interesting to note that the two basic shapes that form a pyramid (a square and triangle) have seven sides—four on the square and three on the triangle—and that there are seven major Chakras or energy centers in the body. Building upon this fact, the Chakramid groups the Chakras into two "Power Packs."

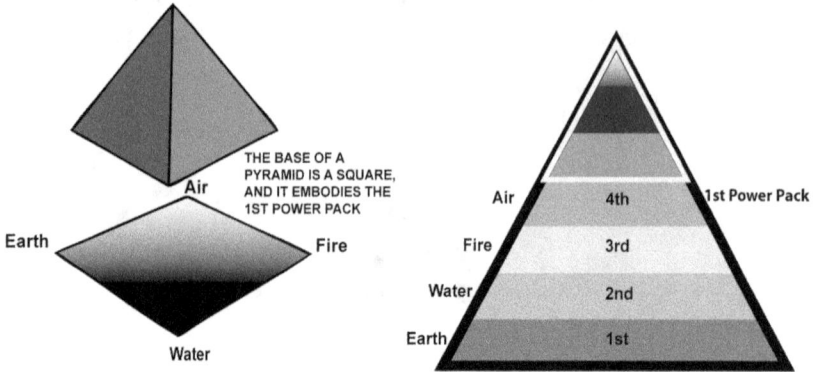

The first Power Pack is represented by the base of the pyramid, and each of its four corners embodies one of the four elements—earth, water, fire and air—which correspond with the elements associated with the first four Chakras. This Power Pack deals with our body from the chest down, and it focuses on our physical, outer energies.

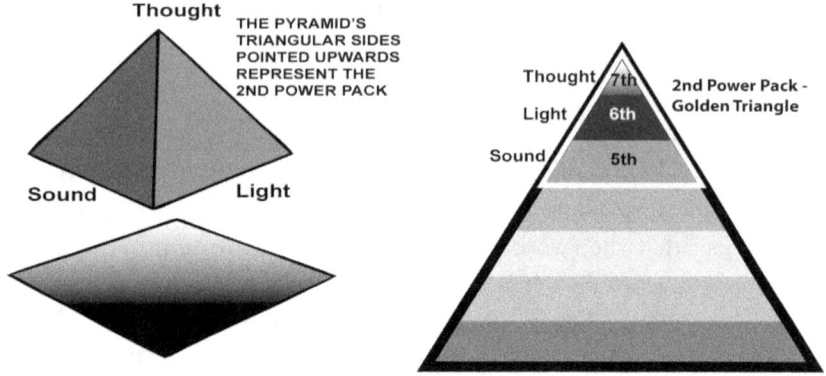

The second Power Pack, signified by the pyramid's triangular sides pointed upwards, focuses on our inner energy. The form of the triangles symbolizes the three elements of sound, light, and thought, corresponding with the last three Chakras. The 5th, 6th and 7th Chakras are often referred to as the "Golden Triangle," which is illustrated by the outline of a golden triangle shape at the tip of the Chakramid. The Golden Triangle represents the way of one's spiritual passage, and each level in it becomes smaller and smaller as one travels farther and farther from the physical, moving towards the barely visible tip and then beyond.

It is also important to consider the way the triangles are positioned in the pyramid. They are perfectly seated and squared on the base, so a stable, balanced foundation is crucial to properly support them. The point of the triangle can be likened to the summit of a mountain, with the ascension of it leading to a higher plane, or to the inner, Higher Self.

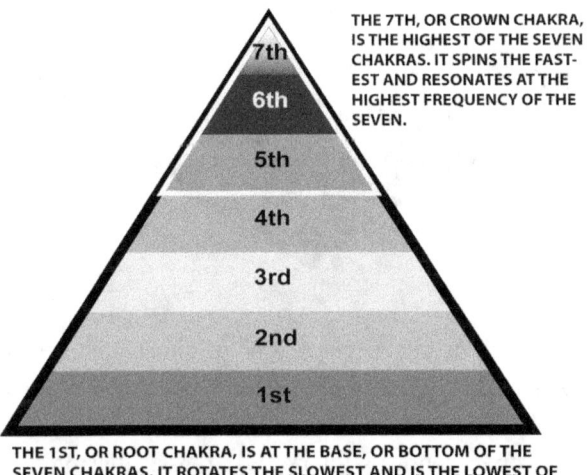

THE 7TH, OR CROWN CHAKRA, IS THE HIGHEST OF THE SEVEN CHAKRAS. IT SPINS THE FASTEST AND RESONATES AT THE HIGHEST FREQUENCY OF THE SEVEN.

THE 1ST, OR ROOT CHAKRA, IS AT THE BASE, OR BOTTOM OF THE SEVEN CHAKRAS. IT ROTATES THE SLOWEST AND IS THE LOWEST OF THE SEVEN VIBRATION FREQUENCIES.

There are several other correlations with our Chakras that lend themselves to our pyramid representation. The colors associated with the Chakras are like stair steps on our Chakramid. The slowest (or lowest) vibration frequency and longest wavelength color, red, is at the base, while the fastest (or highest) frequency and shortest wavelength color, violet, is at the point of the Chakramid. The same observation is true of the sound frequencies often associated with the Chakras. The slowest frequencies are at the bottom and linked with the 1st Chakra, while subsequently higher (or faster) frequencies are at the top. We also find that the first three Chakras deal with the physical world, and they are the biggest, most visible part of the Chakramid. The 4th Chakra begins the transition to the inner, spiritual realms (that you don't see), and the last three Chakra levels become increasingly smaller, until you finally reach the barely visible tip and move beyond it into infinity.

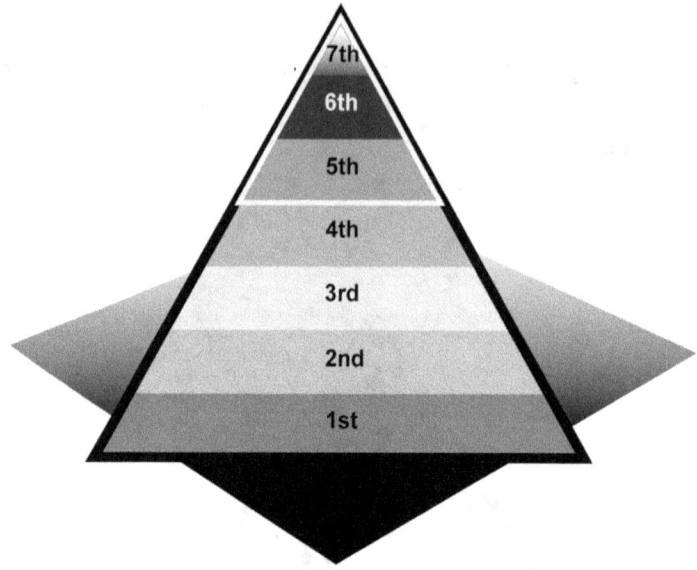

The Chakramid is the perfect way to illustrate one's ascent to the Higher Energy Self through the art and act of working with and balancing the Chakras from the foundation up. When Chakras are balanced, they become clear and open conduits for receiving, assimilating, and circulating energy throughout our entire bodies. The result is vibrant physical health and mental and spiritual well-being.

What Blocks a Chakra?

So how do the Chakras become blocked? Imagine a dam blocking the flow of water. That is exactly how Chakra energy is dammed up as well. Each pent up, unreleased or held-in emotion (such as fear, anger, resentment, or guilt) adds to the barriers that block the flow of energy to or from the Chakra pathway. An unfulfilled need for love and nurturing, especially as a child but also in adult years, can inhibit Chakra energy flow, too. These energy blocks can severely stem the flow of energy, or ultimately build up to the point where they completely close off the energy we receive from a specific Chakra.

Chakra closures most likely happen from the top down as each particular type of energy is blocked. As children experience parental, caregiver, or society's pooh-poohing of anything that smacks of the supernatural (spirits, visions or hearing the unseen), their 7th, 6th and 5th Chakras can become inhibited. Then as they grow up and experience emotional pain and disappointments (such as relationship breakups, failures, letdowns, and stress), all but the first two Chakras can also close, depending upon how those issues are handled. Even the 1st and 2nd Chakras might be affected by those incidents, remaining imbalanced or distorted, and thus hampering their free flow of vital energy.

When our Chakras are out of alignment, severely blocked, or even completely closed off, physical illnesses or mental health issues may occur. The flip side of this is that the same results can also manifest when *too much* energy is released from a particular Chakra. Very often these ailments or disturbances are temporary, but they can persist and develop into chronic conditions. That is why a *balanced* Chakra system is so important.

So it is easy to see how a Chakra becomes blocked and how that can impact us. Now the question is, how do we fix it? How do we open a closed or blocked Chakra?

How Can You Unblock a Chakra?

The good news is that there are innumerable ways to unblock and rebalance your Chakras, clearing and revitalizing them. Some of the tools available to you include (but are not limited to) breath-work, meditation, prayer, journaling, color and sound therapy, gemstone/crystal therapy, yoga, reflexology, Reiki, flower essences, and essential oils. Put a strong desire and a clear intention at the top of your list, and you will find the perfect technique that resonates with the unique being you are.

Another great tool is our Chakramid™ Guided Journal (available at www.Chakramid.com). Its pages ask questions that will help you dig down to the very core of your Chakra blocks or impediments. The book also contains Chakra Rx-ercises (activities prescribed by you!) that can help you create balance in your life.

This is as deep an explanation of the Chakras as we are going to offer here in this little book. Our intent is merely to introduce you to the tip of the iceberg (or shall we say, "Chakramid"!) with regards to the subject of Chakras, and to provide you with just a few methods for getting in touch with and restoring balance to them (if need be) in a fun, fantasy story format. We hope to stimulate your interest in learning more. There is an abundance of expertly written books and web site content available, as well as wonderful classes you can take on this subject. (A list of references is continually updated on our web site, www.Chakramid.com.)

As you begin your journey upward and inward, we wish you many blessings and Godspeed!

1ST POWER PACK

Accepting an Invitation

Jessica had just received something unusual in the mail. She noticed it right away among the customary stack of bills, past-due notices, and junk mail. It was just a plain white envelope with a black outline of a triangle in the upper left-hand corner, but it was the beautiful, elegant handwriting of Jessica's name and address that caught her attention. Her curiosity aroused, Jessica ripped open the envelope. Inside she found an invitation with the same simple triangle at the top. *Is that professional calligraphy?* she wondered as she read the attractively penned invitation.

To her delight, Jessica discovered she had won an all-expenses-paid trip to an exclusive penthouse. "You are assured that your every need will be met, and all your fantasies of a lavish lifestyle will be fulfilled," she read to herself, and then Jessica whooped out loud, "Whoo hoo!" *My lousy luck must be turning around*, Jessica thought, as she checked her calendar for the dates of the reservation and found that she was free to accept the offer.

On the day of her departure Jessica realized that she didn't even know what she needed to bring along for the trip. She looked in her closet with disgust and thought about how much she hated the way her clothes fit her body and how unattractive she felt. After rummaging around a bit though, Jessica finally gathered some things she thought might be appropriate. After all, the invitation promised that her every need would be met—maybe they would buy her a new outfit or two! Jessica haphazardly threw some toiletries and the clothes she had chosen into her bag and then she was on her way.

As she drove following the instructions in the invitation, Jessica noticed she was getting farther and farther away from town. And in fact when she arrived, she was flabbergasted to find that the destination (of all things) was a giant pyramid, sitting alone out in the middle of nowhere. *Well*, Jessica said to herself, *there is that pyramid in Las Vegas. Maybe this is a casino. Surely they would have a penthouse in a casino. That must be what I've won! But I hope they give me some money to gamble with, because with my miserable job, I don't have much to spare.* As she drove closer and closer to the pyramid looking for a parking space, Jessica had to admit that it looked pretty plain and nondescript to be a casino, but perhaps they were putting together a focus group to get feedback before their grand opening, or something like that, she reasoned.

Since there were no other vehicles in sight, Jessica figured there must be underground parking. She stopped her car and walked impatiently up to the only door she could see, with the intention of sarcastically inquiring about how she was supposed to get to the parking garage. As she approached the building, Jessica noticed that from this angle of the structure there were no windows and no doors visible, other than the one she was walking toward. Even the plain, unadorned utility door, which she had just reached, had no windows or markings on it. Still irritated at the inconvenience, Jessica stormed inside and found herself in a long, narrow hallway. It was brightly lit and there was a deep red carpet runner covering the white tiled floor, leading to what appeared to be double doors at the end of the hallway.

I must have come in the wrong entrance, Jessica thought, *but I bet the lobby is behind those doors.* Jessica made the long trek to the doors at the end of the hallway, and as she drew closer, she realized that what she thought were double doors were actually elevator doors. Finally reaching the elevator, Jessica intended to go down to the garage for parking instructions, but there was only an "Up" button available beside it. "That figures," she muttered out loud to herself as she peevishly pushed the button. When the doors slid open, Jessica rushed into the elevator, and they whooshed closed behind her.

With a nervous glance at the closed doors, Jessica thought, *let's get this thing moving,* as she looked around for the control panel. She found it beside another set of sliding doors on the opposite side of the ones she had entered. Despite her agitated mood, Jessica couldn't help but chuckle as she felt an almost overwhelming desire to say, "Beam me up!" The control panel was like no other she had seen before. It was labeled "First Power Pack" and contained four spinning disks. Each disk was a different color and each had a button beside it. The colors went from red up to orange up to yellow up to green.

They all appeared to be spinning at different rates; some were barely moving, and one was spinning at warp speed. That was the red disk. Jessica was reluctant to press the button beside the red disk because she thought it was probably the emergency button. However, it was the only one that was illuminated and she was starting to feel that this may, in fact, be an emergency. She pressed the button and the elevator lurched with a jerk and a bump. It didn't go up, but Jessica was relieved when the doors beside the panel automatically slid open.

Jessica quickly exited the elevator, ready to give someone a piece of her mind, but what she saw stopped her in her tracks. She had entered a very large and virtually empty room. The walls, floor, and ceiling were all white. The only color to be seen was a single horizontal red stripe about one-and-a-half feet high that ran around the perimeter of the room at floor level. *That's it; I'm getting out of here*, Jessica thought, as she stomped back on the elevator through the doors that had remained open. Jessica searched and searched for a button beside the doors through which she had originally entered the elevator, but she could find nothing. Next she turned to the "First Power Pack" panel and tried to press the buttons beside the orange, yellow and green whirling disks, but the elevator wouldn't budge.

Exasperated and a little frightened, Jessica stepped back into the red-striped room as her tumultuous mind was frantically thinking about what to do next. She listened as hard as she could to see if she could hear any sounds in the building, but all she could detect were her own thoughts colliding together in mass confusion. All of a sudden she noticed a wooden chair in the middle of the room. Was it there before? How could she possibly have missed it? Jessica allowed the chair to draw her into the room, all the while looking completely around her to make sure that she was truly alone, because as much as she wanted someone else to be in the pyramid with her, she was afraid that someone or something else was.

Jessica gingerly sat on the chair, making sure that it would support her weight. Why she was worried that it would not was beyond her comprehension at this point, but she was wary of it just the same. Perpendicular from the elevator in the exact center of the room, the chair was facing east. From this perspective, seated in the chair, Jessica was looking directly at a metal-framed canvas with the words, "I have," painted in wide, bold, red strokes on a pristine white background. Now she thought that she was just losing her mind. There is no way she did not see that deep red painting on that plain white wall. How could she have missed it? And what did it mean?

1st Chakra

"I have"

Suddenly, anger overrode Jessica's fear and she shouted, "Okay, I can play this game!" Rage filled her voice as she spewed out loud:

"*I have* a tiny, cramped apartment."
"*I have* an old, junky car."
"*I have* a job that I hate."
"*I have* coworkers who laugh at me behind my back."
"*I have* a fat body."
"*I have* no money and no prospects of getting more."
"*I have* a boring, lonely life."

As Jessica paused to take a breath before continuing on, a picture of her mom and dad popped into her head. Jessica's face softened and her body began to relax a little. Her parents really did love and support her. They had helped her move last year when she had to downsize to a smaller apartment because she could no longer afford her old place. And they did give her a little money to help her out from time to time. Jessica acknowledged that she did *have* loving, well-meaning parents, and she decided to tell them how very grateful she was and how much she loved them as soon as she got out of this godforsaken place.

Just then Jessica was startled by a flash of white light that she saw out of the corner of her eye. She turned and put her attention behind her where she felt the flash had originated and stared in disbelief at what she saw. Standing there as plain as day was a full-length, wood-framed mirror with a garment hanging from it. *Now this is just freaky,* she thought. Jessica nervously surveyed the entire room again and again and still she could see nothing and no one. Slowly, she inched her way over to the illusion—because surely she must be hallucinating—to take a closer look.

The garment was a deep red dress, but it was no ordinary dress. Although she didn't recognize the brand on the label (and she knew them all)—gold threads spelled out "CHAKRAMID"—it was unquestionably an expensive designer garment. *Perhaps the dress was commissioned by the casino,* Jessica thought, and she only hesitated for a second before she quickly disrobed to try on the confection. "Well, if there *is* anyone watching," she said out loud to herself, "they'll be disappointed looking at *my* fat body." As Jessica pulled the dress over her head, she savored the softness of the rich material as it brushed her face, as she slipped her arms into it, and as it drifted down and caressed her body. *That's quality,* she thought, *not like the bargain basement specials I can afford to buy.* But even as she thought the thought, Jessica felt a hot shot of shame, remembering her closet full of expensive articles of clothing that she could not afford to buy when she purchased them with her credit cards. Jessica quipped a flippant "Oh, well," and then promptly dismissed those uncomfortable thoughts.

The dress fit perfectly. As Jessica peered at herself in the full-length mirror, she was shocked at what she saw, so much so that she unceremoniously lifted the skirt of the dress up to her chest to make sure that it really was her body inside. Confirming that it was, Jessica let go of the hem, allowing the dress to cascade back over her body. It clung where it was flattering to her and flowed away from the areas that usually made her tug and pull at her clothing. Jessica did a double take in the mirror, because she could swear she actually looked taller (or maybe she was just standing up a little straighter).

For the first time in a long, long while, Jessica felt good in her skin. She even girlishly twirled round and round as she admired herself in the mirror. When she did that, for some unexplained reason she thought about the whirling red disk in the elevator. Jessica froze in mid-twirl, however, when she saw *the shoes.* Shoes were a particular passion of Jessica's and these were just her style. She quickly kicked off the shoes she was wearing to try on the pair that awaited her by the mirror. As she slipped her foot into each one, she relished the thrill of trying on something new. Generally, Jessica tried to find shoes that she thought made her feet look smaller. She hated how big her feet were, so she often squished her piggies into shoes that were on the small side to get the look she wanted. But these shoes were beautiful *and* comfortable. She loved the way her feet looked in them and she liked the way they supported her as she did a runway walk for the mirror.

After her one-woman fashion show, Jessica decided to sit down in the chair again. Faced with the "I have" painting once more, she thought about how funny it was that the new dress appeared just as she was feeling love and gratitude for her parents. She wasn't even thinking about new clothes, but that dress and those shoes were just what she needed to send her spirits (and self-confidence) soaring.

Jessica's stomach started to growl, reminding her she had skipped her usual coffee and pastry that morning, thinking she would be feasting on a fabulous breakfast. Now she scoffed at the thought. Sitting there alone, however, she admitted to herself that she only bought coffee and sweets at the fancy coffee store because that is what all of the successful-looking people at her office did. But actually, it only made her feel bitter and resentful that she had to waste her money that way for the sake of appearances, when she knew she had overdue bills stacking up back at her apartment. *Wouldn't it be nice,* she mused, *if I could start preparing a quick, delicious, healthy breakfast that would nourish and satisfy me every morning?*

Jessica was so surprised that she almost fell off of her chair as another flash of white light directly in front of her produced a tray overflowing with food. Jessica stared at the bounty that lay at her feet. The tray offered a sumptuous selection of strawberries, red apples, and slices of watermelon. Sprinkled here and there were piles of nuts and seeds. Hard boiled and scrambled eggs and a selection of breakfast meats completed the fare.

Leaning over to pick up the tray, Jessica did a perfunctory scan around the room, not really expecting to see anyone, and she did not. She hoisted the heavy tray up and balanced it on her lap. Surveying the spread, Jessica didn't even know where to start. She picked up a single strawberry—plump and perfect. She took a bite of it, and a sigh of satisfaction escaped her lips as the flavorful morsel met her taste buds. There was no sugar, no whipped cream, no chocolate coating the strawberry, but it was undoubtedly the most delicious berry she had ever eaten. Perhaps it was the silence enveloping her that made her senses so sharp, but as Jessica ate her meal she was profoundly aware of all the smells, all the colors, all the textures, and all the tastes that it offered her.

Jessica ate until her hunger was satisfied and no more. For a moment she thought of stuffing herself, in case there would be no more food that day, or for however long she would be forced to stay in this barren room. But for some reason she was feeling more keenly aware of her red-wrapped body, so she chose to be content with the nourishing portion she had consumed.

As she returned the tray to the floor in front of her where it had originally appeared, Jessica saw a glass of water and a cup of tea. Were they there before and she just had not noticed them? Moving the tray aside, Jessica scrutinized the drinks. She lightly touched the water glass with her fingertips, and it felt cold. She could see that the tea was still hot by the wisps of steam swirling from it. *No, they were not there before,* she told herself. She wondered if while she was concentrating on her meal, she simply did not see the white light that had preceded the drinks, or had they magically appeared without fanfare to meet her needs?

It didn't really matter because Jessica *was* thirsty, and she chose the tea to drink. In her haste to take a sip, Jessica had forgotten to even look for sugar, which she customarily dumped into her tea, needed or not. Each sip of the hot liquid was soothing and comforting to Jessica, and she felt relaxed and warm inside. As she lowered the tea cup into its saucer, she looked at the set: paper thin, perfectly matched, white on white. Rarely did Jessica take time to appreciate the functional items in her life, but here, for some reason, she felt a deep appreciation for the form and function of the cup and saucer.

Not needing one before, Jessica had not contemplated the absence of a bathroom. Well, she needed one now, and she began to wonder what she should do. The familiar feelings of irritation and annoyance began to swell in her again, but something told her there was no need to worry. "Well," Jessica said out loud, "things do seem to appear around here when I put my attention on them, so I will just think about it for a while." *But it can't be too long,* she nervously added to herself. Jessica squinted her eyes with the intent of methodically searching the walls. Sure enough, a few yards away she detected a very, very faint outline of a door that blended in perfectly with the wall. The only real, perceptible thing about the door was the doorknob extending outward from it, although it, too, was white.

Relief rushed over Jessica as she ran to turn the doorknob, fearful that she would not be able to see it again if she hesitated too long. The door opened to the most beautiful bathroom she had ever seen. Everything in it was posh, polished, and perfectly clean. The intricately tiled white walls and floor glistened and sparkled in their spotless state. After she used the facilities, Jessica walked over to the white marble sink, which was adorned with a gold faucet. The sink was centered in a very generous vanity that spanned the entire length of the wall. An expensive looking lead crystal vase held a dozen heavenly-scented, deep red, long-stem roses. Jessica leaned over one of the huge blooms for quite a while, breathing in its sweet fragrance as she gently cupped it between her hands. An ornate crystal pump bottle and a fluffy white hand towel were the only other items to be seen on the vanity top. As Jessica picked up the soap dispenser to admire it, she could detect the same exhilarating aroma that emanated from the roses, mixed with another subtle scent in the background that she could not quite identify.

Jessica's mind wandered as the warm water flowed over her extended hands. Perhaps it was the stark contrast to her own bathroom that made this plain (and some may even say sterile) room so appealing to her. Jessica's bathroom back home was admittedly small, but she realized now that it was the clutter that made it feel claustrophobic. It had a nice size vanity; however, it was overflowing with bottles of lotion (some with hardly a trickle of lotion in them), unused makeup and skin care products she had purchased and did not like, and discarded jewelry she had taken off and carelessly left. She cringed as she thought of the toothpaste and water stains that she had neglected to clean from the sink and exposed sections of the vanity top. As Jessica cast a glance at the shiny white floor below her now, it made her think of the clothing that littered the floor in her own bathroom, which usually stayed there until round-up time on laundry day.

Jessica turned the faucet off and dried her hands on the fluffy white towel that awaited her. After carefully wiping the faucet and surrounding vanity top with it, she folded the towel and returned it to its previous place. Taking one last whiff of the roses, Jessica opened the door and returned to her "cell." She quickly turned to take a look at the bathroom door again so she could remember exactly where it was, but it had already faded into oblivion, which did not really surprise her.

Faced with the prospect of just sitting alone in the wooden chair, Jessica felt a sudden urge to take a walk, which was truly out of character for her. Jessica had half-heartedly tried to stick to exercise goals in the past; recently she had used a popular aerobics tape for a couple of weeks, but it made her knees hurt, and jogging in the park lasted only one day as she could only "jog" for a few yards. But in this silent place, it seemed as though her body was talking to her, as it did before when she ate her breakfast, and now it was saying, "Let's walk!"

So walk she did. Starting slowly, Jessica strolled around the outer edges of the room. Gradually she picked up her pace, and soon found herself walking at a pretty good clip. A picture of a hamster running in a spinning exercise wheel popped into her head, and she chuckled at what someone would think if they saw her parading around the perimeter of the room, swinging her arms, panting slightly, but with a smile on her face. She had lost count of the number of times she had gone around the room, but this time as she approached the southwest corner to the left of the elevator, she saw something lying on the floor. Jessica stopped and bent over to pick it up. It was a spiral bound book. The cover was plain except for a black outlined triangle just like the one on her invitation. However, this triangle was not empty; it had a red stripe inside at its base and the word "CHAKRAMID" was printed in bold black letters beneath it, and underneath that in parenthesis the words, "Chakra Pyramid." "Oh," Jessica said out loud, "It's not a triangle. It's a pyramid." *But what in the world is a "Chakra,"* she wondered, *and why had the book appeared when I was not even thinking about it?*

As was her habit now, when Jessica passed the elevator, she pushed the "Up" button, but as she expected, the doors remained clamped closed. Jessica mindlessly walked back toward her chair as she flipped through the pages of the book. Well, she tried to flip through the pages, but only the first few would turn. The rest seemed to be fused together, and she was afraid that she could not pry them apart without ripping them to shreds. So she turned back to page one, Chapter One, titled "1st Chakra."

With her nose in the book, Jessica lowered herself in the chair without looking, but she quickly sprang back up in surprise when she felt something cold underneath her. Looking down at the seat, Jessica saw a beautiful writing pen. She picked it up, delighted with the gift. The pen's metal casing was sleek and cool to the touch. Its middle section was clear and there was a single, deep red bead threaded on a rod inside. She tipped the pen back and forth expecting to see the bead slide on the rod, but it remained steadfast where it was, as if there was something holding it there. Jessica went to sit down on the chair again, but this time she gave the seat a good look before she did.

As she sat down, Jessica noticed that the water glass was still by her chair, and she picked it up and took a long, refreshing drink of clear, pure, cool water. By the time she placed the glass back on the floor, it was already full again. Jessica was totally absorbed in the book, which she discovered was a guided journal, and her hand was continuously writing—except for a few thoughtful pauses. During those times, Jessica would look up and search her mind and her heart for the answers that the book was extracting from deep inside her. Some of the answers were on the surface, easy to see and write down. But others had to be excavated from depths that Jessica didn't even know existed within her. It was almost as if she were two people: one living her life with quick answers and clinched fists ready to fight and run on a moment's notice, and the other, wiser one who knew the answers to the hard questions, but whispered her wisdom so softly that it required Jessica to put her attention inside herself and listen and listen in order for the pearls to be revealed.

Jessica spent what seemed to be hours reading and writing. Food appeared when she was hungry and the bathroom door faded in and out as she needed it. Now as Jessica stood up from the wooden chair to stretch her tight, stiff body, she casually thought how nice it would be if she were lying on a soft, comfy bed. She was only a little surprised when a flash of white light in the far right-hand corner of the room produced a beautiful bed with the most luxurious, deep rose-colored bedding she had ever seen. With journal and pen in hand, Jessica ran over to the bed, sat on its edge, and then plopped down on her back. Her body sank deep into indulgent luxury. The bed's covering was incredibly soft and smooth. Looking up, Jessica could see that the headboard was upholstered in the same rich rose-colored fabric as the bedding, with deep, deep tufting, unquestionably inviting her to lounge and read in bed. Before she did, however, Jessica wanted to remove her chic, new, red dress and shoes. At home Jessica would have just taken the dress off and thrown it into a corner or left it where it fell from her body. But she had already grown accustomed to the order and harmony this space offered, and she wanted to keep it that way.

Jessica hung her dress back on the hanger that was still dangling from the full-length mirror. As she did so, she took a moment to admire the lovely ornate detailing of the dark wood frame surrounding it. Jessica noticed that the deep red dress covered the mirror almost completely. Her dress was wrinkled and rumpled where she had been holding the book on her lap for so long, but it still looked lovely draping the mirror. She lined up her new shoes underneath it. Next, Jessica picked up and folded her own clothing she had cast off that morning and laid each piece neatly in her suitcase, and then along with her old shoes, she stowed it on the floor under the bed. She had pulled a nightshirt from her suitcase and quickly slipped it on. Looking back toward the elevator, Jessica realized that from this vantage point, the bed was perfectly positioned for her to easily see the entire room, and she felt some comfort in that.

Jessica lifted the gorgeous rose comforter and turned down the sumptuous sheets exposed beneath it. As she slid into the bed, she thought of the phrase in the invitation that promised her that "all of her fantasies of a lavish lifestyle would be fulfilled," and she realized that as far as she was concerned, in this moment, it had come true—she felt like a queen. She leaned back on the deeply tufted headboard and drew the covers up to her chin, gratefully appreciating the richness of the fabric gently embracing her body. Jessica remembered her book, so she picked it up with her pen and started reading and journaling again until she reached the end of the first chapter.

At this point, Jessica was so tired that she did not even mind that she could not go any further in the journal because the remaining pages were stuck together. She put the book and pen aside and began to lower herself in the bed. As she did so, the lights in the room started to dim. By the time her head was resting on the pillow, the room was completely dark. Jessica felt a little afraid at first, but then she eased her mind by remembering the day's activities and the fact that the elevator doors were still tightly shut. (She would worry about *that* tomorrow.)

As if in rebellion to the confines of the plain white room, Jessica's dreams were a kaleidoscope of people, places, and things. She dreamed of wondrous places of enchantment and beauty, and she was guided in her travels by kind, helpful people who seemed to be trying to show her more than the typical points of interest, but that she just could not see. When Jessica awoke from her slumber, she felt rested and revitalized. She stretched her body out as long as it would go and let out a very satisfying yawn. She was ready for whatever this day would bring her.

As Jessica's feet met the floor, for some reason she felt like giving them a little stomp or two. She chuckled as she did it because it made her feel more connected with the ground, something she had never really considered before. Just then an image of the earth spinning on its axis, perfect and protected, popped into her head. She had often silently ridiculed the people in her office who bothered to toss their beverage cans and discarded papers in the recycling bins, and especially the ecology *"green*niks," who ran about crusading against pollution. She always thought what difference could they make? Now she could see the integrity of their intentions to save Mother Earth, who gives so freely of her resources. Jessica thoughtfully made a list of some of the things she could do to help, too (whenever she got back home), in the margin of one of the pages in her journal.

Her thoughts turning to the bathroom, Jessica wondered if there was a shower in there. She had not noticed one before, but then she had not looked for one. On cue, the faint outline of the bathroom door resurfaced. She turned the barely perceptible doorknob and entered the room. The first thing she saw was a huge shower. Its glass doors were transparent portals to a variety of shower heads and wall water jets that promised her a spa experience. Quickly shedding her nightgown, Jessica eagerly entered the shower and reveled in the comfort and joy that the hot water delivered as it washed over her body. A tiny ledge held a bottle of shower gel labeled "Patchouli." Its earthy scent made her feel alive and invigorated. After the longest shower of her life, Jessica reluctantly turned the water knobs off and opened the doors to find a pile of fresh, fluffy white towels at her feet. She wrapped one around her body and turned to the sink.

All of the essentials she needed were lined up neatly on the vanity next to the hand towel. A toothbrush and toothpaste, hair dryer and brush and comb, and razor and shaving gel patiently waited to serve her. After she was done with these items, Jessica noticed two bottles standing against the mirror. The larger bottle was body lotion, which Jessica smoothed all over, paying special attention to her legs, which were just a little sore from her walk yesterday. The second, smaller bottle was identified as foot crème. Jessica was delighted at the idea of giving herself a foot massage, and seeing a small stool under the vanity, she sat down and did just that. Feeling pampered and pretty, Jessica folded her towel and left the bathroom to get dressed for the day.

Jessica walked over to the mirror where her deep red dress was draped. She was surprised to find it freshly pressed and all ready for her. As she took the dress off of its hanger, she could see a reflection of herself standing naked before the mirror. Normally Jessica would have looked away in disgust, abhorring the pieces and parts of her that did not fit her image of a perfect body. But today she gazed at her body as if seeing it for the first time. She noticed that she did have some good qualities: the nice, even tone of her skin; her shining eyes and hair; the graceful curve of her long neck; and, oh, those newly massaged and cared for feet that felt so renewed and rejuvenated (which she had always thought were ugly and too big before).

After slipping the dress on over her undergarments and sliding her feet into her new shoes, Jessica was ready for a healthy morning meal. Midway in the trip to her chair, however, Jessica heard the elevator chime, and suddenly its doors slid open. She very slowly walked over to the elevator, cautiously looked inside, and saw that it was empty. Jessica gingerly put one foot on the floor of the elevator, and stood there straddling between the known and the unknown. Even though she was captive in this space, she had grown to feel safe and secure there. Realizing that it was time to move on, though, Jessica chose the unknown and stepped completely into the elevator car. The doors immediately closed behind her.

Once again facing the "First Power Pack" control panel, Jessica noticed that the red disk was not moving at warp speed any longer, but instead it was twirling at a constant and moderate pace compared to the other disks. It was still illuminated, but now the orange disk was lit as well. However, the orange disk was moving very, very slowly, just barely creeping along actually. Jessica pressed the button beside it and the elevator started its ascent.

2nd Chakra

"I feel"

Jessica's body could feel the sensation of movement as the elevator glided upwards. And as it rose, so did the fear and anxiety in her. *Who am I going to see? Will I be allowed to leave this place? Why am I being held here?* As the shotgun of questions fired off in her head, the calm and peacefulness that had embraced Jessica just minutes before were eradicated by the old familiar feelings of anger and rage summoned to mask her fear. *Why was I tricked into coming to this place? Who do they think they are? How do they think they can get away with this?*

This barrage of thoughts was interrupted when the elevator stopped with a jerk and then rebounded with a little bounce. Jessica held her breath and the inside of her stomach jumped and bounced, too, as she waited for the doors to open. The pause was just enough time for Jessica to ready herself for the confrontation that she anticipated would take place. But when the doors opened, Jessica was astonished by what she saw. She was facing the very room she had just left. Everything was exactly the same: the chair in the middle of the room; the mirror with the empty hanger hanging from it; and the bed, looking rumpled and slept in.

Unaware that she was even doing it, Jessica stepped off of the elevator while incredulously taking inventory of the room with her eyes. And as she did so, the elevator doors slammed shut behind her. Jessica whirled around and frantically pushed the "Up" button, but the doors remained closed. Then she tried to pry the doors apart with her fingers, but they would not budge. The safety and security she had previously felt had not been transported with the room when it made its ascent with her via the orange button. Thinking of the orange button made Jessica aware of the one difference she could detect in the room. The lone red stripe painted on the walls at the base of the room was now accompanied by an orange stripe of the same height painted right above it.

Jessica fearfully scanned the entire room with eyes desperately straining to see who (or what) was behind this cruel joke, but she could see no one. Drawing in a deep breath to let out a scream filled with fear and anger, Jessica suddenly stopped when her attention was drawn to a second canvas hanging on the wall across from the chair. From her vantage point in front of the elevator doors, she could not see what it was or what it said. As Jessica looked down to take a step toward the chair in the middle of the room, she was shocked to see that her deep red dress was now a vibrant orange color. (Her darling new shoes were just the same though.) Putting aside her bewilderment of how this could be, Jessica slowly and cautiously crept toward the chair, doing a full scan of the room as she proceeded straight ahead. When she reached the chair, she placed both hands on the back of it to steady herself as she turned to fully face the second canvas.

The canvas was surrounded by the same metal frame as the first picture and it was hanging in perfect alignment with its partner. The plain white canvas displayed the words "I feel" painted with a flourish in orange paint. Jessica slowly walked around the chair to take a seat. When she sat down, she drew her feet up, resting the very back of her heels on the very edge of the seat, with her knees together and pulled up as close as she could get them to her chest, and then she encircled them with her arms. Jessica tried to clam up her thoughts as she had unconsciously done to her body. She saw no reason to explore her feelings. What use was there in that? Jessica had learned long ago that feelings meant pain, so she protected herself by numbing all of her emotions. The exception was anger, which she relied upon as a close, personal ally to fight any fear that she faced.

With nothing scarier than her own emotions facing her now, Jessica suddenly slammed her feet on the floor and sarcastically yelled out loud "Oooo! Is this where someone is going to get off watching the fat girl cry her heart out?" As if in response to her outburst, a huge picture of her family was projected on the wall right above the twin, framed canvases. At first Jessica just stared at it aghast, but then she quickly spun around in her seat trying to see where the projection was coming from. She could see nothing on the wall, ceiling, or floor behind her that could be responsible for the image she was seeing. Then she looked above her, to the left and right, and finally again to the front of her, and still she could perceive no visible means for the projection of the family portrait.

Jessica stared at the picture for a moment. Well, there she was, bigger than life, looking plain and dull standing next to her beautiful, sweet, older sister, Michelle, who was the pride and joy of her parents. Jessica's parents were seated in front of them and her mother was immortalized in the act of patting her favorite daughter's hand, which rested on her mother's shoulder. Jessica's own hands hung limp at her sides and as she looked at this blown up version of the image, she could see that she appeared to be leaning back slightly, setting herself apart from the close-knit group. Jessica remembered how the photographer kept hounding her to "smile" in response to her quarter moon, tightly closed lips. She shook her head as she wondered how two people who had produced the lovely Michelle could have just two years later created such a disappointment as her.

Michelle was the perfect child—adorable, attractive, and accomplished. She was smart, good at sports, musically inclined, and popular with her peers. Jessica, on the other hand, was none of those things. She struggled in school, was not athletic at all, had no talents to speak of, and was virtually invisible to her classmates. If only she could have gone to a different school instead of trailing along in the wake of the "perfect" Michelle. Maybe then her teachers would not have looked at her with such high expectation in their eyes when they met her. A look that quickly diminished and then vanished completely once they realized she was not a clone of Michelle and they lost interest in her. And all her parents' well-meaning attempts to encourage Jessica to mirror her sister's accomplishments only made their second daughter feel second best.

The present was no different. Michelle had attended college on a full scholarship. She was very successful in her career, was married to a loving, successful husband, and lived in an exclusive part of town teaming with other successful people just like her. Michelle was always inviting Jessica to visit her home just so she could rub Jessica's nose in her success. Her parents could not afford to send Jessica to college, but she didn't know what she would have studied anyway. After graduation, she had held a series of dead-end jobs—most ending in some sort of drama causing her to leave—leading up to her current position as a receptionist for a large accounting firm.

As she thought about her job, the projection of Jessica's family thankfully disappeared. However, in its place was a video of Jessica sitting alone at her desk at work. From the looks of the coffee and sweet roll in the middle of her desk, it was the morning—Jessica's least favorite part of her day, because that is when all of the executives, assistants and other workers come streaming into the office, each of them either completely ignoring Jessica or giving her an obligatory nod or half-hearted smile. As she watched the first few workers walk by her in the video, her face grimaced in horror and she yelled out loud, "Oh, good grief! Don't tell me that I'm watching some perverted version of *This is Your Life,* or something like that!" *Is that what all of this charade has been about? Have they been prepping me for some sort of new reality TV show?* Jessica half expected to see a television show host pop up out of nowhere and start making fun of her and her wretched life, but no one appeared and the video continued.

Jessica tried not to watch it, but she could not keep herself from sneaking a peek to see what was happening. Slowly she became totally focused on the image of herself projected on the wall. From this perspective, she could see that many of the people coming into the office were actually looking directly at her and smiling, and some even said, "Good morning," or "How are you doing?" But Jessica's head was down or her eyes were averted, intentionally avoiding contact with any of them. Jessica gasped as she realized that from the looks of it, she was actually the snob that she thought all of her coworkers were. She was the one who was unfriendly, unapproachable, and uncommunicative. It was her, not them.

At that instant the projection of Jessica in her office stopped, then faded into one of her sitting in her apartment talking on the phone. From the responses she heard herself saying, she remembered a conversation she had had with her sister recently. Michelle had pulled some strings and managed to get tickets to a sold-out concert Jessica had been dying to see. Michelle was always doing things like that just to prove to Jessica that she could. Jessica's first inclination was to gratefully accept Michelle's invitation to go to the concert with her, but something in Jessica made her reject her sister's generous offer. Jessica had fabricated some lame excuse for not being able to make it, because she just didn't feel like giving her sister the satisfaction of feeling superior to her. As the telephone conversation ended, the projection of Jessica faded and was replaced with one of Michelle. Michelle was holding two tickets in her hand, which fell from her grasp as she covered her face and softly wept. Now Michelle's parting words, "I was just hoping we could spend some time together, but I understand," reverberated in Jessica's ears. Why hadn't Jessica heard the sincerity in her voice? How could she have been so cruel?

The family portrait that had originally appeared now returned, but then everyone began to move as it transformed into a video version of the photo session. Jessica watched as the photographer positioned all four of them as she wanted and began checking her lighting before the shoot. Jessica remembered that her mother told her earlier in the morning that the color of her dress perfectly matched the color of her eyes. At the time, Jessica thought it was obvious her mother couldn't think of anything better to say, since the dress apparently made her look fat and frumpy. Jessica could see herself fidgeting with her dress, oblivious to the fact that her mother turned to her, reaching for her hand. Just then the photographer told everyone to face her. Michelle put her hand on her mother's shoulder to comfort her, and when her mother reached up and patted Michelle, the photographer started taking pictures. Jessica felt ashamed when she realized the photographer's pleas for a smile were not intended for her, they were for her mother.

The projection stopped as suddenly and mysteriously as it had started. Jessica hung her head as she began to understand that if this were a reality TV show, it would be called *This is Not What You Thought Your Life Was*. How could she have been so blind to what was going on around her? How could she not have seen the outpouring of love and affection from her family? At her feet Jessica saw two trays; one had a steaming cup of hot water with an assortment of teas and a glass of water, and the other was piled high with muffins and fresh fruit, including orange slices that looked radiant and inviting. Jessica wasn't hungry at all, but she gratefully took the glass of water and drained it before replacing it on the tray. Then she picked up the teacup and mindlessly dunked a teabag up and down in it as she stared straight ahead, mesmerized by the "I feel" canvas. Jessica removed the tea bag from the cup and stirred her tea round and round with a spoon.

For some reason a childhood trip to a wax museum came to Jessica's mind. The trip was a reward for another of her sister's many accomplishments. For this reason, Jessica had been difficult, pretending that she was being dragged along and didn't want to go, when the truth was, she was excited to make the trip and curious about what she would see. Jessica was fascinated with the lifelike forms on display at the museum. Each exhibit was more real looking than the last, and she had an uncontrollable urge to feel one of the characters to see if it felt real, too. Ignoring her mother's demands (and then pleas) to "stay back" each time they came to a new one, Jessica leaned in closer and closer over the velvet ropes that corralled the vignettes, trying to touch one of the wax forms. Finally Jessica had seized an opportunity to dive under one of the ropes when her mother's attention was distracted elsewhere. She distinctly remembered the shock that rippled through her body as her fingers made contact with the wax figurine. And her mother's horrified scream to "stop" was not nearly as startling as what she felt.

In complete contrast to the pretense of life on display, the flesh of the wax figure felt hard, cold and lifeless—dead to the touch. The shock that permeated Jessica's body that day at the museum traveled through her body now as she realized that she, too, had a hard, cold layer covering her body. Jessica dropped her teacup as she fanned her fingers apart and looked at her hands. She could almost see the layers and layers of pseudo protection she had applied to herself each time she felt emotional pain from a real or imagined experience throughout her life. Sitting here alone, she could literally feel the weight of the shell that encased her. It deadened her feelings and filtered her perceptions. She could see now that she had been looking at life through a waxy film that distorted and skewed the way she perceived everything.

Just being aware of it made Jessica want to free herself from the exterior covering with which she had painstakingly sheathed herself, but she instinctively knew it was going to take time to shed that shell. Kind of like a chocolate drop you let melt in your mouth, massaging it with your tongue and letting it soften and dissolve against the roof of your mouth as you patiently wait to get to the nut you know is inside. Jessica burst out laughing as she realized that *she* was the nut in this scenario. It felt really good to laugh at herself, and Jessica decided to get up and move a bit. Glancing at the bed, she noticed it had been made and her journal was lying on top of it. She started walking toward the bed and her journal, but suddenly stopped and put her attention on the bathroom. Breathing in the sweet, uplifting fragrance of the roses would clear her head, and her heart.

As Jessica started to open the barely visible bathroom door, she could see that the room was dimmer than usual and that it flicked with shadowy movement. She hesitated a second, and when she slowly opened the door the rest of the way, her heart actually skipped a beat with delight at what she saw. The shower had been replaced with an antique claw-foot bathtub overflowing with bubbles. Peach-colored rose petals were scattered on the white tile floor leading up to the tubby retreat, enticing her inside. Dozens of candles lit the room, staging a sensual, undulating show on the floor, the walls, and the ceiling. Jessica quickly disrobed, hanging her newly orange dress on a hook on the door and throwing her tired, old undergarments into the corner.

Lowering herself into the tub, Jessica was keenly aware of her body. She almost felt she owed it an apology for the verbal abuse she had given it that morning. Each time she had made a derogatory remark about it in word or thought, Jessica knew she had betrayed the same body she had so appreciated in front of the mirror that very morning. Jessica's body seemed to be thanking her with the heightened sensations she was enjoying in the hot, rose-scented water. A pillow cradled Jessica's head, softening the edge of the tub, and her arms were draped around its sides, totally limp and relaxed. Jessica's nostrils detected the jasmine scent released by the candles, and she gratefully took it in with deep, rhythmic breaths.

For once, Jessica's thoughts were not bouncing around in her head like a ball in a pinball machine, pinging around and setting off bells and whistles for whatever reason. Her mind was as relaxed and at ease as her body, and from deep inside she suddenly knew that everything she saw, heard, and experienced that day had changed her; she was not the same person who had stepped off the elevator that morning. She also *knew* that her emotions were of her own making and that she could choose to see and *feel* the truth in any relationship or situation without judgments or embellishments. In this changed state, Jessica could actually feel the energy flowing through her body; she felt alive, happy, and conscious. For the first time in years Jessica was fully conscious and aware. The delicious feelings her body was experiencing were so sensational because she was in "real time," in the present, in the moment.

After soaking down to her soul, Jessica stood up and reluctantly pulled the stopper from the drain. The water immediately began spiraling downward, creating a mini-tornado that spun round and round. Jessica watched it until the water was gone, and then she leaned over and picked up one of the fluffy white towels on the floor beside the tub. She wrapped her body, stepped out of the tub, and walked over to the vanity. Her beloved roses in the lead crystal vase were replaced with a cheery bunch of birds of paradise tied together with a raffia bow. Jessica loved their exotic beauty, and she imagined that she was at a spa in a tropical retreat. She picked up the bottle of jasmine-scented lotion resting on the vanity countertop and smoothed the creamy elixir all over her body. Jessica blew out the candles, retrieved the orange dress from the hook from which it was hanging, and picked up her undergarments lying in the corner. Mentally cleansed and changed, Jessica felt like writing in her journal.

As she closed the bathroom door, Jessica saw something orange lying on the bed next to her journal. She walked over and squealed with glee at what she found. Laid out on the bed were the most gorgeous, satiny, lacy bra and panties she had ever seen! They were tangerine colored and intricately detailed with a flower motif. Jessica would never even dare to look at the "pretty" underwear whenever she went shopping for fear that someone would make fun of a person of her size looking at such delicate, sexy items. Jessica threw off her towel and put on the pretties. She walked over to the mirror and stared at herself. Her breasts looked positively perky in the bra, and the panties lovingly hugged her hips with a clean, smooth line. Looking at her womanly, curvy figure, Jessica felt sexy and desirable. Sensual Latin music started playing in her head and she danced to it in front of the mirror, totally free and uninhibited. Jessica felt fabulous!

Goosebumps covered Jessica's body, although she did not feel cold, so she decided it was time to put on her dress and take a look at her journal. Jessica hated to cover up her lovely new lingerie, but she reveled in the richness of the orange dress fabric as it slipped over her body. Jessica picked up her journal and pen at the foot of the bed and was surprised to discover that the lone deep red bead decorating her pen now had an orange companion nestled right next to it. She examined the journal's cover as she climbed into the bed and rested her upper body against the soft, spongy headboard, and she noticed the pyramid now had a new orange stripe right above the deep red one at the base of the shape. Jessica's brow furrowed a bit as she flipped through Chapter One, stopping to read any phrase that stood out and flagged her attention. When she came to the end of the chapter, she found that although the pages to Chapter Two were no longer stuck together, the rest of the book was still not available to her. Thoughtfully balancing the weighty pen in her hand, Jessica intently read the content on the first page of Chapter Two and then started to write in the journal.

Jessica wrote and wrote, and as she did, sparkling water, teas and juices appeared on a tray to satisfy her voracious thirst. She repositioned her body whenever it felt uncomfortable or stiff, but she remained fully focused on the task of excavating and exploring her feelings. It was often physically painful to feel the feelings that had been blocked, lying dormant in her body for so long, and many a tear was shed. Exhausted and prodded by hunger pangs reminding her she had not eaten that day, Jessica decided to take a break. Getting out of bed, Jessica stretched her body upwards as far as her hands could go, and then she stretched to the right, down towards the floor, to the left, and then completing the circle, back up towards the ceiling. She stamped her feet and a huge smile warmed her face. Jessica felt wonderfully alive and grounded.

Jessica walked over to her chair in the middle of the room. The light repast that appeared at her feet was a veritable feast for the eyes. A brightly colored citrus salad, a creamy squash soup spiked with a pungent, fragrant spice, and a sunny dessert soufflé graced the tray Jessica now balanced on her lap. Wanting to leave the exploration of her life behind her for a while, Jessica put her full attention on her meal. As she mindfully ate, Jessica's senses came alive, and she was fully present for every taste, every texture, and every smell that she gratefully received from the food. When she was pleasantly satisfied, Jessica replaced the tray on the floor and it immediately faded away. Once again she sat facing the "I feel" painting, but this time it did not strike terror in her heart. Instead, she actually felt sorry for the person who had previously sat is this chair alone and aloof, because although she was certainly still alone, she was no longer detached from her feelings. She knew that her healing would be a process, but she also knew she was finally on the right path.

Jessica felt tired and worn out, so when she returned to her bed (or her throne, as she thought of it) she readied herself for the night, taking off and hanging up her prized orange dress and underwear. But she did not put on her nightshirt; tonight she slipped into bed completely naked, and the luxurious bedding felt soft, soothing, and sensual to her skin. Jessica picked up her journal and just stared at the page. Maybe the real reason she decided to take a break stared back at her. This section of the journal was asking about her love life. Well, there wasn't much to probe here. Jessica's romantic relationships could be counted on two fingers and each was short and ended unpleasantly. The sexual encounters that ensued from them were strained, awkward, and completely unsatisfying. Thinking about it now, however, it was easy for Jessica to see she was incapable of giving anyone the love, respect, and attention that she couldn't even give to herself.

At this point the journal was asking Jessica to describe her perfect mate, and her pen unwaveringly recorded a description of the man of her dreams. This exercise took Jessica to the end of Chapter Two, and she laid her pen and journal aside and sank down into the lavish comfort of the bed with the lights dimming in sync with her descent. Mentally and emotionally exhausted, she immediately fell into a deep, restful sleep. As happened the night before, Jessica dreamed of exotic places, but this time she was in a tropical haven filled with birds of paradise and gorgeous looking men who could see the beauty in her, inside and out. And once again she was joined by friendly, helpful guides who seemed to want her to see something she could not.

When Jessica woke up, she felt as if she had been reborn. Recharged and reenergized by the night's restful sleep, she felt prepared and eager to begin this fresh new day. But first, she lay in bed just a while longer and stretched out her body as far as it could go; holding the stretch for several minutes, she made note of every part of her physical body and flowed appreciation to it. Releasing the tension, Jessica allowed her body to relax completely before getting out of bed. Standing by the side of the bed, Jessica put her chin on her chest and slowly curled her upper body down as far as she could go. She straightened back up very slowly, one vertebra at a time. She couldn't explain it, but Jessica felt lighter and more flexible than she had ever felt before.

Walking over to the mirror, Jessica carefully removed the hanger with her freshly pressed and cleaned orange dress and pretty undergarments suspended from it. Then she proceeded to the bathroom, intent upon taking a refreshing shower. When Jessica entered the bathroom, she hung the hanger on the hook on the back of the door and glanced at the birds of paradise on the vanity countertop. They were like old friends, and she could have sworn that she saw them waving their orange wings in greeting to her, and she jokingly waved back to them. Jessica turned on the shower faucets. (The bathtub was nowhere in sight.) Stepping inside, she savored the massaging force of the hot water as it pulsated against her body. She picked up a bottle of jasmine-scented foaming shower gel from a tiny floating shelf in the shower and leisurely washed her body with the moisturizing bubbles. Stepping back into the flow of the water, Jessica watched the bubbles as they slid down her body and formed a foamy circle above the drain going round and round before they dissipated and finally disappeared.

Turning off the faucets, Jessica picked up one of the warmed, soft, white towels waiting for her and dried her body with it. She walked over to the mirror and looked at herself. She felt an urge to put her hands on the lower part of her stomach below her navel, and as she did, she could feel that it was relaxed and calm. However, in the upper part, she felt the sensation of butterflies fluttering around inside, the way she felt when she anticipated that something scary or something exciting was about to happen. Jessica went about her usual morning routine readying herself for the day, which now included the rituals of mindfully moisturizing her body and massaging her feet. Then Jessica happily put on her sexy underwear and slipped into the cheerful orange dress. She glanced around the bathroom one last time to make sure everything was picked up as she turned the knob and opened the door. Jessica was not at all surprised when the elevator bell chimed just as she closed the bathroom door, and that the elevator doors opened wide, patiently waiting to receive her.

3rd Chakra

"I act"

Looking at the open elevator doors, Jessica hesitated just a minute and then turned in the opposite direction. It was not fear that made her head for the farthest point from the waiting transporter; there was something else she wanted to do first. Jessica pulled up the sheets on the bed and neatly tucked them in and then she smoothed out the gorgeous rose bedcovering, making sure it was evenly distributed all around the bed. She started to lay her journal and pen at the foot of the bed, but reconsidered it and put the pen in the book and tucked it under her arm. Now she was ready to go.

Jessica resolutely stepped into the elevator this time. There was no wavering between the known and unknown. She had changed and she suspected that the process was not complete yet. Just like a caterpillar curled up in its cocoon, Jessica felt she had only just begun her metamorphosis. Facing the First Power Pack again, Jessica could see that the orange disk, the second on the control panel, was now spinning smoothly and in sync with the first red disk. The next illuminated rotating disk ascending up the panel was bright yellow. Its behavior was wildly erratic, intermittently going from a turtle's pace to a harried hare's. Jessica pushed the button next to it. As the elevator smoothly took off, Jessica put her attention on her dress and then looked at the cover of her journal. Her dress had already turned a sun-drenched yellow, and the pyramid on the front of the journal had a new yellow stripe above the orange and the red ones.

When the elevator stopped and did its little bounce, the butterflies in Jessica's stomach fluttered to her attention. Jessica placed her hand on her stomach just above her navel as the elevator doors opened. She was not surprised to see that her room had once again made the trip along with her. Looking at the wall next to the elevator, Jessica ran her hand along the additional yellow stripe. Its sunny color was warm and alive. Remembering the two pictures on the wall opposite her chair, Jessica put her attention there and confirmed that the twin pictures had become triplets. She walked over to the chair, casually glancing around the room as she went. As she sat down to study the new message, a perplexed look took over her face. In sweeping yellow strokes the words, "I act" were painted on the stark white canvas.

Jessica's baffled eyes now reflected a blank stare. For her, taking action usually meant something was going terribly wrong. Jessica lived her life in a status quo state until some new situation or event came up that forced her to react to it. Like looking for another job because she was let go from a previous position, or moving to a new apartment because she could no longer make the payments on the last, or even shopping at a different grocery store because the one she frequented had closed down. Jessica started to feel uncomfortable and somewhat afraid that those two words meant something bad was about to happen.

The instant that thought entered her head a scene from her life began to play out on the wall above the trio of pictures. Jessica was sixteen, and she was standing in front of her class reading from a paper clenched in her trembling fingers. "Oh, no," Jessica said out loud, "I don't want to see this!" She averted her eyes, trying to concentrate on something else…anything else, but like a magnet, the video kept pulling her attention to it. "It's like watching a train wreck," Jessica whispered. It was a writing assignment she was reading. The homework was to write creatively on any subject and in any format the student chose. Jessica had labored over a poem that literally bared her soul. In figurative terms each verse told the tale of her life and how she felt. When she was done reading, Jessica shyly looked up, only to be confronted by the indifferent gaze of her peer group audience. Worse yet, some of the boys were rolling their eyes at each other and snickering under cupped hands covering their mouths. Jessica was devastated, and she remembered later that night crying in her room and vowing never to open up like that again; she would never again take such a chance, because her experience proved it would only lead to failure, shame, and disgrace.

Jessica was fully absorbed in her 16-year-old self and reliving those painful moments in her bedroom when something flickering in front of her brought her back to the present. She looked up and saw that the video was focusing on someone else in the classroom. Her name was Renee, and she was one of the popular kids who would never even dream of talking to Jessica. But she was not smirking or laughing. Actually, she was looking down, and her bottom lip was quivering like she was desperately trying to compose herself. Jessica remembered that Renee had brushed by her after class that day and snidely remarked, "Nice poem." But as the video continued, Jessica could see that Renee actually sought her out when the dismissal bell rang, touched Jessica's arm to get her attention and sincerely said, "Nice poem." And then ever so softly, "I know how you feel." The video abruptly ended with those words, leaving Jessica gaping at a blank space on the wall.

Jessica sat still for quite a long time, but her mind was racing with questions. *Why didn't I hear Renee's whispered words of appreciation and understanding? How could I have mistaken such obvious sincerity with sarcasm? If I had realized that I had touched even one other person with my written words that day in school, would the tears I had shed in my room that night been tears of joy rather than tears of shame? How would my life have been different if I had not made a pact with myself that night to never act so rashly again?* It was that last question that left Jessica motionless for so long, as she thought about the string of safe, but futile, jobs she had held since high school.

Jessica was suddenly aware of her parched lips and a tray with a huge glass of water appeared at her feet. A large lemon slice was balancing on the edge of the glass, and Jessica removed it and squeezed its pungent juice into the water before she took a long, satisfying drink. As she leaned over to put her glass back on the tray, she saw that it now offered a steamy cup of water for tea, packets of granola, bananas, and a serving dish piled high with very generously-sized whole grain muffins that her nostrils could tell were laced with cinnamon. Jessica picked up a napkin and one of the mammoth muffins and ate, slowly savoring its earthy texture and spicy taste. When she was full, she returned the rest of the muffin to the tray and picked up the cup of hot water and a tea bag. As she steeped the tea bag in the cup, transforming the water into a delightful brew, she wondered what was next for her that day. As if on cue, the wall before her started to project another segment of Jessica's life, and Jessica slumped back in her chair, mortified when she realized what was coming next.

Jessica considered her current job boring on its best days and demeaning on the worst. Her duties include answering the telephone and greeting guests, along with some other trivial tasks handed off to her from time to time. But although Jessica was the lowest person on the organizational chart, she was president and CEO of the lobby, and she sometimes wielded her power with a harsh and heavy hand. Jessica had invented a game she called "Power Play," the object of which was to throw players off balance and put them in their place. The video in front of her was projecting a particularly unpleasant round, which had taken place recently. Generally Jessica saved this pastime for people she considered to be inordinately arrogant or pushy, but for some reason the pretty, poised woman who came into her lobby that day was targeted as an unknowing and unwilling participant. She had pushed the lobby door wide open with pronounced confidence and assurance. Jessica immediately knew the designer of the very expensive suit she was wearing, which for some reason annoyed Jessica and made her want to "put the woman down a peg or two."

The woman approached Jessica, offered her business card, and stated who she was there to see. It was a scheduled meeting, which Jessica knew concerned a new national advertising campaign for her company. It was a big contract and there were several contenders vying for the prize. She was early, so Jessica told her to take a seat and then announced the woman's arrival over the telephone. She returned the phone to its cradle and told the woman that her party was busy and would be with her as soon as possible. The woman took a seat and her hand rested on a large portfolio she had pushed back next to her chair. Jessica casually asked if she was there for the advertising contract and the woman smiled and nodded her affirmative answer. Jessica advised her they had already seen several excellent presentations that day, and then leaning forward she added in a softer, confidential voice, that she had overheard they had already picked a favorite and that was who they were spending so much time with right now. The woman shifted uneasily in her seat and her fingers visibly tightened around the portfolio. After a few minutes had passed, Jessica smugly noted that the woman nervously began tapping her foot and then groped around in her purse, finally producing some note cards that she was quickly leafing through. Mission accomplished. Game over. Jessica's ego swelled.

Managing a slew of telephone calls that were suddenly coming in had Jessica's full attention, so she did not notice when the previous presenter was ushered out of the conference room and the woman was invited in. Later, Jessica overheard two executives discussing the woman they had just seen, as they were leaving for lunch. "That last woman certainly presented the best portfolio of ideas, but I just don't think she has the confidence to handle a national campaign like ours," one said. The other replied, "You're right about that, she barely even looked at us throughout her entire presentation!" Jessica remembered thinking at the time that it probably would not matter to the woman anyway. Surely someone like her had lots and lots of opportunities lined up just waiting for her.

The video suddenly stopped and comically began rewinding everyone backwards. It continued until Jessica could see the woman backing into the elevator. The video stopped there and then started playing forward again at that point. Jessica saw the woman carrying her portfolio off of the elevator. When she found the right door, she leaned the portfolio up against the wall next to it and took something out of her jacket pocket. Jessica could see that it was a photograph of an adorable little girl with a huge, open smile. The woman looked at the photo for a moment and then said, "This is for you and me, baby. We're going to make it on our own." Then she kissed the picture and returned it to the safe haven of her pocket. Drawing in a deep breath, the woman picked up her portfolio and resolutely pushed opened Jessica's lobby door.

Jessica sat motionless for a second, and then she literally flung her body from her chair and ran over to the elevator. She frantically pushed the elevator button, pleading for it to open, but it did not. Jessica pressed her back against the wall next to the elevator, and as twin streams of remorse and regret flowed from her eyes, she slid her body down until she was sitting on the floor. She tried to restrain her feelings, but the floodgates had been opened yesterday and she knew she could never go back to the shell of herself she had relied on before to thwart off emotional pain. Jessica jumped up and started walking. Her legs were moving as fast as the thoughts were flying around in her head. *Why did I make up that stupid game? How could I have done that to that poor woman and her child? What is wrong with me?* Suddenly from deep inside, Jessica distinctly heard the words, "Shut up and just walk!"

Jessica resisted the directive at first, caught up in the drama of the moment. But she finally decided to concentrate on her surroundings instead of her crisis in order to calm herself. As she walked, Jessica looked at the walls and noticed their smoothness, the intensity of the three colors banding the room, and the brilliance of the white space above them. Then she looked at the floor, invoking the same process. After she had been playing *this* game for a while, Jessica did feel calmer and more composed. She slowed her walking pace and headed over to her chair in the middle of the room. The video was frozen at the point where she had bolted from her chair. Jessica knew she had to finish the clip, but not now. She glanced at the bed in the corner of the room and discarded that as an option, as well. Then she put her attention on the bathroom. She didn't have to use the facilities, but now it seemed like a refuge, a safe place where she could sort out her feelings.

As Jessica cracked open the bathroom door, she noticed the same flickering movement inside as the day before when the antique claw-foot bathtub had appeared. But Jessica did not feel like soaking in the tub right now; she just wanted to sit and think. Jessica pushed the door all the way open and caught her breath at the sight she saw. The bathroom had transformed into a meditation room. The vanity was in the same place, but it was lower to the floor and had an alter-like appearance. The sink in the center of it had been replaced with a fountain—a multi-tier rock formation with water springing from the top and spilling over the rocks below with a gentle, relaxing sound. Seven large, white candles surrounded it, and their undulating, fiery tips were mesmerizing. An ornately carved teakwood box held a stick of Cinnamon incense that offered its scent in smoky swirls. The crystal vase remained, and it held a bouquet of radiant yellow carnations. A single, round yellow cushion on the floor was perfectly centered in the middle of the room, enticing Jessica to sit.

Jessica closed the door and sat down on the cushion with her legs crossed at the ankles, not quite like the pictures she had seen in magazines where perfectly-shaped women had both feet on their opposite thighs, but she figured it was close enough. She had never meditated before and really didn't even know what she was supposed to do, but sitting on the cushion this way, taking in her surroundings with all of her senses made her feel good. Baroque music started playing gently in the background. In her outside world Jessica never would have sat still and listened to classical music, but in this space she could actually feel the melodic tones playing inside her as they softly, yet intensely floated in the air. Jessica closed her eyes and just sat. She thought she was supposed to try to think of nothing, but no matter how hard she tried, thoughts kept popping into her head. After quite some time had passed, she eventually began to realize that her past was in the past, and that her power was in the present—this moment, here and now. Jessica was ready to see the rest of the video that was waiting for her, so she stood up, blew out the candles, and went back to the chair facing her gallery.

As soon as Jessica sat down, the frozen video began to fast forward past the part she had already seen, and then it abruptly stopped and focused on a scene showing the two executives who had passed her desk that day discussing the woman. They were with the woman now, and she was profusely and gratefully thanking them for the opportunity to handle their advertising campaign. She added that she didn't think she even had a chance after the receptionist in the lobby had told her they had already picked a favorite. One of the men asked her to repeat that last statement, which she did, and he said he would deal with that employee when she returned to the office. Jessica's heart sank as she realized she would not be welcomed back at her job, but she felt better knowing she had not ruined the woman's chance to work on the advertising campaign.

The video faded out and then faded in, this time focusing on the laptop computer in Jessica's apartment. It zoomed in on an email in her "Deleted" box and just stayed there. The email was from the editor of a popular women's style magazine, to which Jessica was a regular contributor on its online message board. Jessica's passion was fashion. She loved everything about it—the clothes, the bags, the jewelry, and especially *the shoes*. Jessica was particularly good at predicting trends. She had a gift for it really, always seeming to intuitively know what was going to be the next "it" thing. Numerous other fashion fans who posted on the magazine's message board actually sought Jessica out, asking her opinions about new styles and fads and what *she* thought of them before the magazine could even get its predictions in print. Jessica's growing following and her obvious wealth of knowledge about the fashion industry did not go unnoticed, and the magazine's editor had recently sent

Jessica an email inviting her to visit their office in New York to discuss the possibility of her writing a monthly column for their print magazine. As soon as she had read it, however, Jessica had exiled the email to her "Deleted" file, not wanting to even contemplate such a scary, daunting thought.

What Jessica was really afraid of was reliving the look of disappointment her accomplished sister's teachers gave her when they realized Jessica was not what they thought she was—a mirror image of Michelle. Did Jessica look like a fashion expert? No. Could she afford to buy the beautiful clothes about which she wrote so passionately? No. Well, sometimes—actually, more often than she could afford, she used her credit cards to make such purchases. But she was also often inspired to create her own fashion designs on the little sewing machine in her apartment. Her happiest hours were spent sewing up her own creations, and she was overjoyed when someone would ask her where she was lucky enough to find her outfit. Of course, Jessica always felt they were omitting the words "in your size," but she enjoyed the flattering attention anyway when she responded that she had designed it herself. Maybe she should retrieve the banished email and make an appointment to meet with the magazine editor. In her current jobless state, what did she have to lose? And maybe, just maybe, she could finally be passionate about her work!

The projection of the email faded away and Jessica sat facing a blank space above the trinity of pictures. Jessica remembered her journal, which she had placed on the floor by the chair earlier that morning, so she picked it up, eager to write down her thoughts. The third chapter of her Chakramid Journal was freed up now, and she noticed that the pen, which she had put at the end of Chapter Two, now had a yellow buddy next to the orange and red beads. Jessica read the Chapter Three introduction before she put pen to paper, and it helped her to put the 3rd Chakra in perspective with what she was about to write. As she wrote, Jessica lunched on a delicious black bean soup accompanied by crusty, grainy bread. And she drank cool, pure water spiked with lemon, and later, steamy hot peppermint tea.

Jessica made her way through all of the questions in Chapter Three of the journal and then it invited her to make up her own. Dozens of blank pages were provided in the book for her to do so. Faced with the blank pages,

Jessica decided it was time for a bathroom break. Besides, she was curious to see if the restroom had reverted back to its former state. As the familiar faint outline of the door appeared, Jessica placed her hand on the doorknob, turned it, and pushed the door open. She was greeted by the brightly lit, gleaming white bathroom. Jessica used the facilities and then turned to the vanity to wash her hands. The crystal vase on the vanity top now held three huge sunflowers with wide black eyes and yellow petal lashes. Just looking at them uplifted Jessica's spirit and made her smile. Before she left the bathroom, she stared one of the sunflowers in the eye and asked it why she was resisting the blank pages in the journal, but in her heart she already knew the answer.

Jessica was always asking herself questions. In fact, there was a constant parade of queries marching around in her head, generally in response to something that was happening, something she anticipated might happen, or something that had already happened and she was reliving. But the basis of her inquiries was always to determine what was wrong with her, to seek out and confirm imperfections, defects, weaknesses and limitations. The blank pages in her journal were an invitation for Jessica to make a complete shift in her thinking, and therefore, in her life. Jessica knew she had come to a crossroad and that the way marked "Why?" pointed to the old, familiar, safe path she was already on, and the other path moving towards a new, exciting, unexplored life was marked "Why not?" Here and now, Jessica had the power to choose which path she wanted to take. Walking to the middle of the room, Jessica bent over and picked up her Chakramid Journal and pen, still resting on her chair where she had left them. She decisively sat down, turned to the first blank page in the book, and wrote, "Why not go to New York, wow them with my fashion knowledge and know-how, and write a monthly column for a highly regarded women's style magazine?" Jessica's pen flew as she began to design a new life for herself.

Much later, exhausted but happy, Jessica ate her evening meal in bed. She dined on lemon pepper chicken complemented by a wonderful yellow, orange, and red pepper chutney, perfectly seasoned brown rice, with a slice of hearty banana bread for dessert. She ate until she was delightfully full and then pushed the food away. Jessica sat still in bed, propped up against the soft, plump headboard for a long time, not really thinking about anything in particular, just appreciating her surroundings. She put her hand on her midriff where butterflies flew that morning. Now it felt peaceful but strong, and she imagined a yellow disk inside her in perfect alignment with the orange and red disks below, all spinning at a moderate, smooth pace. Keenly aware of the upper and lower sections of her stomach, Jessica climbed out of bed, stretched and limbered up her body, and then did some stomach crunches on the floor. She could only do a couple reps, but the physical exertion felt great after the mental workout she had had that day.

Lying a little breathless on the floor, Jessica mused that like a butterfly, she had shed her cocoon that day, emerging to flex her wings, preparing to fly. She realized that floating along with a breeze instead of fighting to fly in the face of it was the way of a butterfly, which was the best way to get where a butterfly wanted to go. But she also knew that *she* had the free will to decide on her path, to reach whatever heights she was aiming for, to choose which breeze she would ride. Jessica felt as free and as light...well, as a butterfly! At that moment she sensed something cool lying against her chest. Her hand automatically went up to touch it, and she felt a chain around her neck with something hanging from it. Jessica sat up to examine the pendant and discovered it was a butterfly with its wings stretched out ready to fly, just like her. Jessica was delighted with the gift and silently and sincerely thanked its giver.

It was time to rest, and Jessica disrobed and carefully hung up her dress. Then she threw on her nightshirt and gratefully slid in between the plush sheets and snuggled down into her bed. She fell asleep almost as soon as her head met her pillow, with fingers wrapped around the butterfly on her necklace. Jessica's dreams were filled with skyscrapers, fashion shows, and butterflies. Her guides were there, too, but this time she distinctly heard one of them say, "Forgive," and then she awoke. She lay in bed contemplating the word for a while. The feelings of anger, resentment, and, yes, even hatred had run so deep in Jessica for so long, that just thinking about the possibility of letting go of long-held grudges and bitterness made her feel lighter. But how could she forgive after all of these years? Jessica shook off those thoughts for now and enjoyed a good morning stretch.

Jessica slid out of bed and mindfully felt the sensation of her feet meeting the floor, and she gave them a little stamp. She put her arms above her head as far as they would go with her hands back to back. Then slowly and deliberately she pushed her arms apart going out and down, and as she lowered her arms, she imagined that she was pushing away any resistance that she felt about forgiveness, until they met her sides. Then she raised her arms back up, mindfully feeling the energy in her body and her newfound power radiating from her fingertips. Jessica raised and lowered her arms like this several times, and when she was done she chuckled to herself, realizing she must have looked like a butterfly exercising its wings.

Making the bed was becoming a morning habit for Jessica. It made her feel centered and grounded to keep her room neat and tidy, she thought, as she finished the task for the day. Jessica gathered up her things and headed for the bathroom door. As she entered, she looked for the sunflowers on the vanity. The cheery bunch was still huddled together in the clear crystal vase, and one of the wide-eyed beauties winked at her, and she laughed and winked back in return. Jessica took a long, hot shower using the lemon-scented shower gel that was offered. Its pungent, powerful scent made her feel that way, too. After her shower, Jessica quickly patted herself dry and then applied the body lotion located on the countertop. It had the same citrusy smell as the shower gel, and she breathed in deeply, appreciating its fresh fragrance. Jessica took a few more minutes to massage her feet with an herbal cream, and then she busied herself with everything else she needed to do to get ready for her day. As she slipped into her sunlit yellow dress, she wondered what this day would bring. She put her hand on the upper part of her stomach and this time there were no butterflies, just a warm, balanced feeling. Jessica closed her eyes and stood still with a quiet mind for a few moments before opening the bathroom door. The elevator was already opened and waiting for her.

4th Chakra
"I love"

Jessica stepped into the elevator and immediately turned to the First Power Pack Control Panel. The first three disks—red, orange and yellow—were all spinning smoothly at a moderate pace. The fourth and last lighted disk, which was emerald green, was spinning very slowly in comparison to the others. As Jessica pushed the fourth button, she felt a little sad to think this was the last leg of her journey. The fourth-disk ride was smooth and uneventful, and the doors opened as soon as the elevator car bounced to a halt. Walking out, Jessica looked down just in time to see her dress transform from sunny yellow to emerald green. She liked the soothing new color; it reminded her of nature—green grass, rustling leaves, and garden vegetables.

Jessica put her attention on the gallery wall. She noticed that the first three pictures were still grouped together like the three musketeers, but now a fourth framed canvas joined them. It was perfectly centered above the other three, and this positioning lead Jessica to believe that the fourth and last message was probably the most important. Walking over to the wall, Jessica could see the green words, "I love," painted in graceful letters. The metal-framed white canvas was perfectly accented by the green stripe on the wall behind it. When she arrived at the wall, Jessica raised herself on tip-toes and reached up to trace the letters with her index finger. As she casually walked over to her chair, she realized she had expected the painting to say, "I forgive," as the guide had advised her to do in her dream.

Reaching the chair, Jessica sat in the seat facing the gallery and her stomach started to growl. Looking down at the floor for her morning tray, Jessica was delighted with the green "fruit fest" she found. There were sliced green apples, pears, kiwi, honeydew melon, and grapes, which were accented here and there with a sprinkling of nuts and petite whole grain muffins. Jessica leisurely enjoyed her meal and then sipped green tea from her white china cup. She sat in her chair feeling full and satisfied. Setting her cup and saucer aside, Jessica looked straight ahead above the lone canvas, and the video started to roll.

Jessica was startled and disturbed as she watched as a man, towering over a boy of ten or so, slapped the boy's freckled face, leaving strawberry stripes on his cheek. Then the man unbuckled his belt while telling the boy to turn around, which the boy reluctantly did, and Jessica flinched three times at the cracking sound of the belt as it cruelly met the boy's backside. "I'm not raising any losers. Do you hear me, boy? I told you not to be daydreaming out there. Do you hear what I'm saying, Tom? You have to focus on winning and nothing else." The man turned and stomped out of the room, and the boy flung himself on his bed. He had tried as hard as he could to throw, catch, and bat the ball that day, but it was not good enough for his father. He softly cried and uttered a vow that he would never hit *his* kids. Then wiping his eyes with his sleeve, he whispered that he would do better, that he would try harder, that he would not be a dreamer—he *had* to be a winner.

The video stopped just then, but Jessica did not even notice. She had never met Tom's father. Her grandfather had died before Jessica was born and her dad never spoke of him. The boy had been true to his word and he never hit his kids; however, his critical words were as stinging as a slap, and they cracked as loud and cruel as a belt. The video continued on. Jessica's dad had signed her up to play softball, something in which she had absolutely no interest. She could not throw, catch, or bat the ball, although she really didn't even try to. But her dad had told Jessica that she must follow through on what she had started, that she couldn't be a quitter. And after every practice and after every game, her dad, Tom, as the video showed, would be in her face yelling at her to do better, to try harder, to stop daydreaming—she *had* to be a winner. And after every practice and after every game, Jessica added a new layer of protection to her heart—her outer shell.

The scene faded out and repeated itself, this time focusing completely on her father yelling his litany of rules, preaching his sermon of winning. Jessica wondered why she had to see the same thing all over again. Anger started to swell up in her chest. *Wasn't it bad enough the first time?* The view panned out and Jessica was surprised to see that it was Michelle who was on the receiving end this time. Michelle was a natural athlete. She excelled at every sport she tried, but she was particularly gifted at softball. In fact, that skill had earned her a full-ride scholarship to a prestigious college. Why was Tom yelling at her?

Jessica studied her sister's face as she endured the tirade. Her expression went from looking vulnerable and hurt to determined and firm. After her father left her room, Michelle threw herself on her bed and wept behind cupped hands. Behind her finger fortress she whispered, "Why can't I be more like Jessica, so silent and strong? She is a daydreamer and she doesn't even care who knows it." And then she shook her head and cried, "But I'm not as tough as her and besides I don't even know how to dream any more." And then Michelle uttered a vow never to bully *her* kids. She whispered that she would do better, that she would try harder, that she could not be a dreamer, so she *had* to be a winner. The video stopped and Michelle's image slowly melted away.

Jessica sat in her chair stunned and amazed. Michelle had mistaken her emotionally anesthetic state—her heart-protecting outer shell—as strength and conviction. But that couldn't have been farther from the truth. In reality, it was just taking the easy way out. It was cowardliness personified and put on like a shield. But Jessica now knew that it was a defense mechanism she didn't need anymore. She had learned to allow herself to actually feel her feelings now, be they good or bad. And she knew that feelings were just things to be experienced for however long or brief a period of time as Jessica chose. So in this moment, Jessica allowed herself to fleetingly feel the pain the video delivered in order to learn its lesson, and then move on.

Jessica turned her thoughts to her big sister, Michelle. Jessica's heart ached for the little girl who lay crying on her bed, deciding to be the best at all costs, betraying her true self for a shadowy replica that could not dream. Jessica could see that winning was Jessica's emotional heart defense of choice, and she wondered if her sister was truly happy with her winnings: the perfect job, the perfect mate, the perfect home, the perfect life. At the end of the day, was Michelle content and fulfilled with all that she had? Or did the price for being the best at all costs weigh down upon her the same way Jessica's outer shell had finally become too heavy for her to bear? The empathy Jessica felt for her sister was pure and true. Jessica's heart swelled with love for Michelle, and she mentally gave her a warm hug she hoped her sister would feel wherever she was. The video started up again, this time with a scene of Jessica receiving the gift of a china doll from her maternal grandmother. Jessica put both of her hands on her solar plexus—instinctively covering her 3rd Chakra—mentally preparing and strengthening herself for the funeral she was about to attend. A part of Jessica was going to die.

As a child, Jessica loved dolls. She would spend hours bathing, dressing, combing, and imagining when she was with them. The china doll Jessica's grandmother had presented to her for her birthday was the prettiest doll she had ever seen, let alone had ever hoped to own. She bear hugged the doll and fervently thanked her grandmother over and over. But her grandmother's reply was to admonish her to take care of the doll because it was expensive, and she took the doll from Jessica and put it up high on a shelf in her bedroom saying, "There, that way you can see it, but not touch it. It's a collectible, not a play thing." To young Jessica that statement was an oxymoron (although she had never heard that word before); how could a doll *not* be a play thing?

For weeks Jessica only toyed with the doll in her mind. She imagined how she would restyle her tight ringlets into softer, contemporary curls. She carefully studied the doll's coloring and came up with a pallet of complimentary colors for her. And she envisioned the perfect new dress for the doll, something with a fitted bodice that gradually flared out and flowed down to its hem. Jessica drew the dress over and over again, re-coloring and redesigning it until she got it just right. Finally, the allure of the doll was too tempting for Jessica to bear, so she dragged a chair from the kitchen into her room and climbed up on it in order to reach the prized collectible. Jessica slept with the doll that night and when she woke up the next morning she had a brilliant plan. Since everyone was always so proud and happy with Michelle when she showed off her talents, whether it was playing softball, soccer, or any sport really, or with bringing home all of the A's that adorned her report cards from school, Jessica imagined how proud and happy they would be with her when she showed them she was talented, too! She might not be able to play sports, and she never did that well in school, but she *could* make this doll look even better than she did now; she *could* make this doll even more collectible!

Jessica knew her grandmother was coming for dinner that Sunday, so she set about working on her plan. Starting with the doll's hair, she cut off the ends of the coiled ringlets and brushed them out until they framed her face in soft, wavy curls. She colored her fingertips and toes with a marker so they would perfectly match the dress she was going to create. Then she started on the dress. Jessica stripped the old-fashioned outfit from the doll and carefully wrapped paper pieces around her for a perfect fit before she cut and colored them. When all of the pieces were painstakingly finished, she glued the bodice pieces to the doll and attached the free flowing skirt to it with more glue. It took a full week to complete the project, but Jessica had never been so proud of herself. The doll was just as perfect as she had envisioned!

Jessica had wanted the timing to be just right for her to show off her handiwork, so she waited until they had returned from watching Michelle's soccer game (where she made the winning goal, of course) to unveil her creation. That was the scene the video on the wall was projecting now. There she was, little Jessica, bringing out her dolly for everyone to see, thinking that she was about to reap the rewards of her talents. Jessica looked at her own little face and wondered if she had ever been happier than that moment in her entire life. When Jessica's grandmother saw the doll, she stood frozen for a moment processing what she was seeing, and then she exploded. She ripped the doll from Jessica's hands, threw it on the ground, and screamed in rage, "Why did you ruin your doll, you ungrateful little brat?" Jessica could see herself, horrified and motionless, and then her grandmother turned on her mother.

"I keep telling you what a terrible mother you are. Look at this mess. Look at what your daughter has done. You don't discipline her enough. She's always wasting her time playing with those dolls, dreaming her life away, and you just stand by and do nothing. She's no good at school, no good at sports, no good at anything! With you as a mother, it's a miracle Michelle has turned out as good as she has. She's the only good thing you've ever done in your whole life. But you'll probably screw her up, too." In the video, Jessica could see that her mother's head was down as her mother spat the words at her, but she quickly looked up at Jessica when her grandmother mentioned Michelle. Jessica's mother looked like she was about to say something, but she just bowed her head again in submission. What her mother had perceived was Jessica standing strong, being defiantly emotionless. But in truth, Jessica was almost unaware of what was going on as a new protective layer was covering her aching heart. Jessica's grandmother ordered her tearless granddaughter to bed without supper. The video focused in on the doll and Jessica could see now (as she had seen then) that its face had cracked, leaving a horrible gaping hole in her forehead.

The video faded out just then and faded back to Jessica, curled up, sleeping in a fetal position on her bed. The door to her room slowly opened, and Jessica could see that her mother held a tray in her hands. She entered the room, and when she saw that Jessica was asleep, she crouched down and set the tray on the floor next to her bed, sat down beside it, and began to stroke her daughter's hair. The tray held a plate full of Jessica's favorite cookies (freshly baked), a glass of milk, and her doll. The doll's face no longer had a gaping hole in its forehead. It had been glued back together, marred but whole. Then Jessica's mother whispered to her, "Baby, you are so tough. You are so strong. Don't ever change. Don't ever back down. Don't be like me." And with her hand still on her daughter's hair, she buried her face in the bedcovers and wept.

The next scene showed Jessica waking up with the doll next to her. Jessica remembered the horror she had felt when she saw its scarred face, and she had fleetingly wondered how it got there. Staring straight ahead, her movements slow and deliberate, Jessica rose up out of bed. In this zombie state, she removed some toys from a box in her room, shredded some construction paper into it, then gently placed the doll in the cardboard coffin and interred it deep into her closet, never to be exhumed. Seeing the scene from her current perspective, Jessica knew she was burying more than the doll that day; a piece of her was in that box, too. A place deep inside her heart was gone—turned off, tuned out. No one in her family ever spoke of the doll again.

The video abruptly ended as Jessica stood up. Her heart felt heavy and weary and she wanted to get away to renew herself, so she put her attention on the bathroom door. As she turned the doorknob and started to push on it, Jessica could feel a puff of warm, moist air hit her face. She extended the door the rest of the way open and stood in the threshold with her mouth agape at the wondrous scene her eyes were beholding. The restroom no longer had conventional boundaries—there were no walls and no ceiling. The floor was a dirt path winding through a tropical rain forest. She could literally see the air as it hung in a hot, heavy haze. Jessica hesitated to enter the scene for a moment as it occurred to her that she might get lost in this place. Then she chuckled very softly as she imagined herself leaving a bread crumb trail to remind her which way she had come. No, she had wanted renewal, and she instinctively knew this was just what the doctor (or she) had ordered. She stepped inside and the door vanished behind her into the mist.

Once inside, Jessica took several deep breaths, enjoying the heavy, earthy smell of the forest's floor mixed with the light, sweet fragrance of its tropical flowers. The flowers poked their heads up here and there, peeking at her over thick emerald green foliage. Branchless tree trunks extended up as high up as Jessica's eyes could see and then disappeared into a massive canopy of leaves and vines. Jessica slowly moved forward on the path, all the while taking in and appreciating the natural, unrestrained beauty that surrounded her. As she passed by, the large emerald green leaves that bordered the path bobbed and waved their approval with her progress. After a short while, Jessica found herself standing before a fork in the path. She stood there for a moment carefully surveying each choice, but when she realized that the leaves themselves actually seemed to be pointing to one way, she decisively took it without giving the other option another thought.

Jessica continued on, enjoying her meandering walk, and she gradually became aware that the peaceful drone of the forest sounds were punctuated by the rhythmic patter of falling water directly ahead. She hastened her pace, making her way to a small clearing that set the stage for a breathtaking waterfall. It was flanked on three sides by a sentry of emerald green bushes, vines, and trees that had worked their way into the rocky habitat, patiently standing guard. The water wall cascaded into a pool, which appeared to be deep in the middle, yet became increasingly shallow and still as it widened out to its rocky banks. Jessica could see there were actually two sources of water at the top of the falls, and they commingled together before dropping into the pool below. She made her way to the stone wall over which the water flowed, and there she quickly stripped off her dress and beautiful new emerald green undergarments and hung them safely out of the way on an extended tree branch. Only the butterfly pendant remained, hovering over her chest. As Jessica stood in the waterfall shower, she imagined it washing away the heartache of the morning's video.

After quite some time had passed, Jessica emerged from the downpour feeling renewed, revitalized, and ready. It was time to do what last night's dreamy guide had whispered in her ear. She was going to forgive. Walking over to the branch where she had left her clothing, Jessica saw a stone bench underneath it, with her Chakramid Journal and pen resting on top. A quick glance confirmed that the pyramid on the cover of the journal revealed a new green stripe and the pen had another emerald-colored bead next to its yellow, orange, and red counterparts. Jessica noticed that the clear barrel of the pen was still partially empty, and she wondered what that space was for. Returning her attention to the task at hand, Jessica dressed and then sat down on the stone seat. She folded her hands in her lap and gazed straight ahead at the twin source of the falling water, and suddenly, she knew what loving and forgiving were all about.

Forgiveness was simply letting go of the past. Not in the zombie-like state in which she had buried her doll, but in a very conscious, deliberate, and, yes, even loving way. It helped to see her parents as wounded children living out their lives, unconscious of the strings still attached to them from the darkness of the past, twisting and pulling them this way and that in the present. They were doing the best they could, but they were stuck in their own separate dramas, dancing to tunes that played over and over in their heads. Being sucked up in their vortex, Jessica had in turn created her own drama, complete with a tune she had been slow dancing to up to this point. She could clearly see the viciousness of the cycle, but she could also see she had a choice to stop it now.

Walking to the edge of the pool, Jessica bent over and picked up four stones. She threw one into the glassy stillness of the pool's border, and mentally forgave her father as she witnessed the ripples emerging from the stone's drop site, emanating out wider and wider until they gradually disappeared. She easily did the same for her mother. Forgiving her grandmother was harder for Jessica until she realized that her grandmother had her own story, her own tune to which she was mindless dancing, and even though Jessica didn't know what it was, she imagined that it must have been horrible. So she threw a stone in the pool for her grandmother and sincerely and lovingly forgave her for her trespasses. Jessica felt a little foolish forgiving Michelle. She had only been trying to bond and have a relationship with her little sister, but Jessica threw in a stone for her anyway, just for good measure. Then she watched the ripples that resulted until there were no more.

Jessica knew it was time to go, but first she spent several minutes in stillness, soaking up the beauty and energy of her surroundings. Remembering her Chakramid Journal and pen, Jessica retrieved them from the stone bench; she had so much to write about and she could see herself doing just that in the luxury of her sumptuous, soft bed. As she turned to leave, Jessica saw a group of butterflies floating in front of her. Their wings were adorned with every color of the rainbow: from bright reds, oranges and yellows, to vibrant greens, to majestic blues, purples and white. They all seemed to be flying in a tiny whirlwind for a moment, going round and round in a flurry of colors and patterns. Then a single butterfly with gorgeous green bands accenting its black wings broke the formation, and the rest followed as they all fluttered toward the path that would take Jessica back to her room. As she began to walk, Jessica realized how light she felt. It was as if her feet were not even touching the forest floor. It was as if she had her own wings, and she was flying home, too.

Jessica dutifully followed the butterfly parade until she could see the outline of her door ahead. When she saw it, she turned and stood still, impressing a picture of the beautiful, tranquil haven in her memory so she could envision and visit it in her mind whenever she wanted. The green and black butterfly came into her view, and she put her hand out with her palm up and it lighted on the little landing pad. Jessica slowly brought her hand up to eye level and she smiled at the butterfly and thanked it for her safe passage. It fluttered its wings twice as if in response and then flew away as the rest of the butterflies followed, bobbing up and down in a lively, multicolored procession. Jessica watched them with a smile on her face until they were out of view, and then she turned to the door and went back into her room.

Even with the four bands of color at their base, Jessica blinked at the brilliance of the white walls as she entered the room. She was hungry, but she couldn't wait to open her journal to chronicle what she had learned that day. As she walked over to the bed, she could see a tray already there waiting for her. It held a big leafy salad, dotted with a variety of vegetables—green peppers, celery, cucumbers and onions. There was dressing for the salad in a gravy boat with a silver ladle on the side, along with incredibly thin slices of meat and chunks of fragrant cheese. Jessica kicked off her shoes, hopped into the bed next to the tray, and gratefully relaxed against the supple upholstered headboard as she ate and reflected on the day's events. Jessica felt as excited as an archeologist discovering the missing link in the evolution of mankind. But what she had exposed concerned the evolution of love, and the missing link she had discovered was forgiveness. However, it did not take a pick, an ax, a spoon or a brush to unearth this great discovery. All she needed to do was lift her chin and open her eyes to see the truth of the waterfall—that when streams of love and forgiveness come together, they transform into one continuous flow of unconditional love.

Jessica could clearly see that the past had choreographed her life up to now, but it was time to let her heart do its own dancing from here on out. Yes, she had forgiven everyone in her life for what they had done to her, but that was not enough. With her heart leading the way, Jessica would be free to love unconditionally with gratitude, appreciation, and forgiveness every day. She would be grateful for her family members and appreciate them for who they were now, not withholding her love until they were the way she wanted them to be. Fortified by forgiveness, Jessica would reclaim her power to choose not to repeat grievances over and over in her mind, not to be offended by what others mindlessly said, not to take everything personally, not to be hurt, not to be wounded. Essentially, Jessica would forgive not only her family, but people in general for being themselves as they live out their lives in varying degrees of consciousness—from fully aware to virtually unconsciousness (the way Jessica had been before she entered the pyramid). Finished with her food and drink, Jessica turned to her Chakramid Journal and eagerly started at the beginning of Chapter Four.

Jessica poured her heart out as she turned page after page and wrote and wrote. She was exhausted, but she fought off sleep to record one last thought. Her eyelids were too heavy to stay open, though, and still dressed and propped up against her headboard, Jessica drifted off to dreamland. Her slumber was filled with visions of the rain forest, the waterfall, and of herself floating free form in the air, gleefully rising and falling with the wind and finally coming to rest in the pool of the falls. There she was met by a beautiful blue butterfly that flew above her in circles. Its wings were fully extended as it rode the current of a tiny whirlwind over Jessica's head. Going round and round it slowly descended downward until it was just inches from her face. Then the blue butterfly landed on Jessica's shoulder and proclaimed the word, "Truth" in her ear. With that, Jessica awoke; the word still ringing in her head.

Jessica lay in bed for several minutes contemplating that single word— Truth. She had already learned the lesson that the video had presented to her about how even simple lies can negatively impact others in unseen ways. So she was wondering if the butterfly's utterance was just a reminder to her as she left this place to always tell the truth. Jessica enjoyed a good morning stretch as she thought about leaving the pyramid. She had ascended to the highest level in the First Power Pack in the elevator, so she assumed that today she would be going back down, back to the real world. She was surprised when she realized how sad leaving this place made her feel. In such a short time this tiny space seemed more like home to her than her four-room apartment.

As Jessica continued to lounge in bed, she shifted her awareness to her breathing. She was lying on her back with her pillow underneath her head. Her arms were straight at her sides and her legs were stretched out evenly on the bed. She began noticing where her breath started in her body, and she followed its movement as it flowed, making her tummy inflate as she inhaled and deflate as she exhaled. As Jessica continued observing her breath, she became more and more relaxed and mindful of her body. In this state, Jessica slowly and fluidly slipped out of bed. Then she made the bed, focusing all of her attention on every minute detail of the activity. When she was done, Jessica picked up her shoes, headed to the bathroom door, and went inside.

Jessica took off her rumpled emerald green dress that she had slept in and hung it on a hanger swinging from a hook on the back of the door. Then she draped her green undergarments over the hook and enjoyed a long, steamy shower, using Ylang Ylang-scented foaming gel. After her shower, she swathed herself with a fresh white towel and walked over to the vanity. The sparkling crystal vase held a Zen group of bamboo stalks, looking stark but sophisticated in their simplicity. Jessica performed her morning rituals of moisturizing her body with lotion and massaging her feet. As she turned to remove her dress and underwear from the hanger, she saw that they were fresh, cleaned, and pressed. Jessica dressed herself as she looked around the bathroom for the last time, and then she opened the door and headed to the elevator.

Halfway to the elevator Jessica remembered her Chakramid Journal and pen. She ran over to the bed where she had placed them that morning so she could take them home with her. As she picked up the book, she realized there were a number of pages still stuck together, and she wondered why that might be as she walked across the room. The doors to the elevator were closed, so she pressed the single button on the wall to open them. They immediately opened and Jessica stepped right in. Turning around, she sadly took one last look at her room as the elevator doors closed together. Jessica put her attention on the First Power Pack control panel. All four of the disks were illuminated and three of them were spinning at a moderate, even pace. However, the fourth disk, the green one, was moving slightly slower. Jessica looked for a down button, but she could not find one. Then she tried pushing the bottom button with the red disk (the first level), but the elevator did not budge. So she tried the orange button and then the yellow, but she still did not move. Just then, the elevator doors slid opened.

Looking down to step out of the elevator, Jessica saw something lying on the floor directly in front of it. She stooped down to take a look and saw that it was a smooth, polished rock. It reminded her of the stones she had thrown in the waterfall pool, and suddenly Jessica knew what she needed to do. Standing in front of the elevator, Jessica cleared her mind, and then envisioned the rain forest. She recalled the sights, the sounds, the smells, and the sensations of it, and then she was there. Jessica immediately headed toward the waterfall. There were no forks in the dirt path this time; she knew exactly where she was going, and she arrived at the waterfall clearing in no time at all. Jessica stood for a minute taking in the majestic beauty of the waterfall, and then she went over to the edge of the pool and threw the stone into it. This time as the ripples emerged and fanned out, she forgave herself for all of her misdeeds, for all of her mistakes, and for misunderstanding what life was truly about. She watched the pool with eyes filled with tears of joy, until the pool was as still as glass again. And finally, for the first time in her life, Jessica felt totally free.

The dinging of an elevator bell brought Jessica back to her room, and she found herself standing in front of another elevator right beside the one she had exited moments before. The doors were already open, encouraging her to enter. Glancing at her Chakramid Journal, she knew there was more to come, so without hesitation, Jessica stepped into the new elevator.

2nd POWER PACK

5th Chakra

"I speak"

After the doors closed, Jessica saw that the control panel in this elevator was labeled "Second Power Pack." There were only three buttons in this power pack, but like the first elevator, there was a spinning colored disk beside each button. The first disk was blue, the second was indigo and the third was violet. They were all spinning rather slowly compared to the disks in the First Power Pack, and Jessica was sure that the fourth disk in that pack, which had been spinning a smidgen slower, was now perfectly in sync with the other three. Jessica reached out her hand and pressed the first button, which was next to the only lit-up disk, the blue one, and she started her ascent. When the doors opened, Jessica stepped back into her room, which was sporting a fresh, new, sky blue stripe painted above the others on the walls. She quickly looked at the gallery wall and saw a new painting was floating above and one space to the left of the fourth picture, which was in the middle by itself. As she walked to the center of the room toward her chair, she could see that in blue letters it said, "I speak."

When Jessica reached her chair, she glanced at the seat before sitting down and noticed that her dress was still emerald green. She also saw something lying in the middle of the seat. She picked it up and felt its cool smoothness. It was another flat, oval shaped polished stone, but this one had the word "Love" carved into one side and the word "Forgive" carved into the other. Jessica was delighted with the gift, which would be a constant reminder of her commitment to unconditional love, and she silently thanked her benefactor. As she sat down on her chair, Jessica's dress turned a very pretty shade of sky blue that perfectly matched the paint on the new canvas and the fifth stripe on the wall.

Jessica was starting to feel a little hungry, and as soon as the thought entered her mind, her breakfast tray appeared on the floor at her feet. She leaned over and picked up the tray. Blueberries were the theme of the morning's meal. There was a crystal cup full of blueberries in cream, nestled between warm multigrain blueberry muffins and whole wheat blueberry pancakes drizzled with honey. Jessica ate slowly and mindfully as she savored every tasty, healthful morsel that passed her lips. Her hunger was satisfied very quickly though, and she returned the tray to the floor as soon as she felt full. The pot of tea she found there was fragrant and steamy, and she picked it up with one hand and the white cup and saucer with the other and poured herself a cup. After several sips, Jessica rested the cup and saucer in her lap and looked straight ahead at the wall, waiting for the morning's video presentation.

Since nothing was appearing on the gallery wall just yet, Jessica patiently began raising the cup to her lips when someone said, "There won't be any more videos." Startled at the unexpected intrusion, Jessica fumbled her teacup like a football and the hot liquid flew out, covering the front of her dress and her lap. Jessica quickly stood up as the cup and saucer crashed to the floor, but the broken bits immediately reassembled themselves and then faded away. She looked all around the room to see who had spoken the words, but no one could be seen. Nervously looking at her seat before sitting back down, Jessica spotted a cloth draped across it. She gratefully picked it up and started using it to wipe off the front of her heavenly blue dress, which had been doused with most of the tea. Jessica noticed that her dress immediately dried wherever the cloth touched it.

As she carefully wiped and dried her dress with the cloth, Jessica heard the same feminine voice as before saying, "You have transitioned from the physical realm of the lower Chakras, and now you can begin your spiritual journey." This time Jessica could clearly tell that the voice was emanating from her person. Her free hand flew up to find the transmitting device, and the first thing she felt was the chain hanging from her neck. "The voice is coming from my butterfly pendant," Jessica whispered, as she cupped the pendant in her hands and anxiously waited to hear more. In the silence that followed, Jessica glanced up at the gallery wall, and she instantly knew what the positioning of the pictures meant. The first three Chakras, represented by the red, orange, and yellow canvases, dealt with the physical world. The 4th Chakra, symbolized by the green picture elevated above and centered over the bottom three, did not denote more importance, as Jessica had originally thought (although it was an extremely important part of her awakening). The 4th Chakra facilitated her transition to the upper level, which begins with the fifth canvas hanging right over the bottom left red painting, and it apparently deals with more spiritual matters.

Developing her spiritual side had never been important to Jessica. Fragmented memories of pontificating preachers were part of her unpleasant childhood memories. Every Sunday Jessica's mother would take the girls to church with their grandmother. There, they listened to tortuously boring, monotone sermons that were periodically interrupted by vehement passages from the preacher or hissing threats from her grandmother to "be still." Jessica never felt spiritual there, but quite frankly, she was often scared when she actually listened to the promises of hell and damnation the preacher delivered. Not quite ready to delve into her spiritual side (and a little shaken by the thought that her necklace was talking to her), Jessica decided to escape into the bathroom.

The white door handle appeared on command and as Jessica pushed the door open, a ray of sunshine gleaming from within spilled onto the floor in front of her. Jessica flung the door wide open to a farmhouse porch, complete with rocking chairs and a pasture view. She quickly stepped onto the porch, leaving the dark thoughts of the past behind her as the door handle faded from her grasp. Jessica surveyed the view and her spirits lifted and soared just like the birds she could see flying over the field. Jessica was a city girl, but the peacefulness and tranquility of this space made her feel like she belonged there. Jessica joyfully stepped over to one of the rocking chairs and took a seat. At first she sat straight up, peering over a whitewashed wood railing the way a child would, excitedly taking in every detail. But after a while she relaxed her body and sank into the comforting form of the chair, and began rocking herself back and forth in a rhythmic flow. Jessica closed her eyes and softly hummed a lullaby to herself. She felt blissfully relaxed, comforted, and safe.

Gradually, Jessica became aware of something brushing against her right hand, which was resting on the arm of the rocking chair. She slowly opened her eyes, blinking at the brightness of the sunshine, and saw the blue butterfly from her rain forest dream perched on top of her hand. Its feet were solidly planted on her skin, but the butterfly's wings expanded outward and then clapped together several times as if in greeting to her. Jessica slowly moved her hand, bringing the butterfly closer to her face and said, "Hi, there! Imagine meeting you here." The butterfly opened and closed its wings together once more and then flew up above Jessica, and as she leaned her head back to see where it went, the blue butterfly fluttered round and round in circles above her. The butterfly suddenly broke this pattern and then flew over and landed on the railing beside her. After a second it took off again, stopping on a flower a few feet away and then went to another a few feet from that. Jessica was not even startled when a voice whispered from the butterfly pendant floating around her neck, "You know what you need to do."

Yes, Jessica knew the blue butterfly wanted her to follow it, but she was reluctant to leave this lovely place, and weren't there wild animals and other dangers to be wary of on farms? Brushing these limiting thoughts aside, Jessica knew she better get moving before she lost the chance to see what she was supposed to see, so she regretfully left the sublime comfort of the rocking chair and started singing "Old McDonald" out loud as she descended the porch stairs in pursuit of the butterfly. Jessica's little blue friend flew at a slow, ambling pace, so she was able to enjoy the journey along the way to their destination. They passed a picturesque, red bank barn (that from the sounds of it housed chickens and goats), a huge bountiful garden tended by a friendly looking scarecrow, and rows and rows of golden tasseled corn stalks. The butterfly abruptly veered off of the path they were on and headed to a clearing to the right of them. Jessica could tell there was something in the middle of it, but she could not quite make out what it was. As she moved closer, Jessica realized that the object in the clearing was a well. A *wishing well*, she thought, as she recalled the phrase in her invitation that said "all of your fantasies of a lavish lifestyle will be fulfilled."

Jessica walked up to the wishing well and carefully leaned over it to look inside. It was very deep and dark in there, so she could not really see much of anything. She picked up a rock from the ground, dropped it down the well, and after several seconds was rewarded with a deep, rich sound as the rock plunged into water. Jessica sat on the stone edge of the well, and slightly leaning over, shyly spoke her name into its depths. The well echoed "Jessica" back to her, so she more daringly shouted, "I love this place," and those words reverberated inside, too.

Jessica then boldly yelled, "I wish I had a million dollars," which was repeated in the well...but then followed with, "But I would probably foolishly blow it all in a year."

Taken aback by the unexpected rebound, Jessica almost fell inside the well. The echo sounded like her voice, but *she* didn't say those last words! Frightened, Jessica was ready to flee, but instead she demanded, "Who's in there?" Her question was echoed back to her and then the answer, "I know." was added.

After a brief pause, in which Jessica was speechless, the echo in the well went on, "What *would* I do with a million dollars?"

Jessica hesitantly sat perched on the edge of the well, ready to leave. Was she really going to continue talking to someone she did not know and could not see? But the question from the well sparked something in her, and Jessica blurted out, "I would buy all of the designer clothes I want and then get them professionally altered to fit me perfectly. Oh, and I would buy lots and lots of beautiful shoes. I would buy a brand new, big and expensive car. Then I would buy an upscale condo in the best part of town with tons of closet space. And after that I would invite my entire family over to see how well I have done for myself."

Jessica's wish list echoed in the well, and then an unasked question followed, "How does that sound?"

Jessica thought for a second and then she said, "Well, actually it sounds like I would blow all of the money in a year and then be right back where I am now."

Jessica's words were echoed in the well much softer now, but the next question rang out loud and clear, "What do I *really* want to do with a million dollars?"

Jessica shifted her weight, finding herself as uncomfortable with the way she was leaning over the well as she was with its last question. Just as she did so, the butterfly pendant on her necklace said, "You know, you don't have to sit on the edge of the well and shout in order to be heard."

"What do you mean?" Jessica said.

"The well is just a symbol for the real well inside you. You can call it a wishing well if you like, but a better term might be your '*Well of Being*,' because it is actually your inner *Self* that you are talking to; it is your higher *Self* that you are getting in touch with."

Just then the rocking chair from the farm house porch appeared beside the well with a side table that held a pitcher of lemonade. Jessica could see that a fresh glass had just been poured. The water-beaded glass contained sparkling ice cubes and was garnished with a sprig of mint. Jessica left her well perch and sank into the familiar comfort of the rocker, then gratefully drank from the lemonade glass, refreshing her parched throat.

Jessica closed her eyes and contemplated the last question from her *Well of Being*. "Well," she said, "I could stay in my own place and be a freelance writer for fashion magazines. I would love doing that and I could help people decide what to buy every season. I could pay off all of my bills, buy a new fuel-efficient car, and maybe see if I can find a larger apartment after that. And maybe I could buy a designer outfit now and then (with shoes to go with it, of course). That way I could be safe and comfortable."

Jessica paused to consider how this wish list sounded—if it rang true and if it felt right. It did, but from deeper within her she heard another question, "What else?"

"Well, I would be free to create my own designs and I would have the money to produce my first line by myself."

She paused and then heard the same question again, "What else?"

"Well, actually, I've been thinking about finding a way to let people know what I have been learning about the Chakras. I am no expert, but I want to share what I do know."

"How?" was the next query.

"Well, I think there might be a way I can incorporate what I've learned into my clothing line. For example, I could use the colors of the clothing and maybe some tags explaining the corresponding Chakras and tips for balancing them. And maybe," Jessica continued as her voice grew more and more excited and engaged in what she was saying, "I would start a web site where people could come to learn and share their experiences, knowledge, and views on their Chakras." As the intensity of Jessica's enthusiasm mounted, she could literally feel her body emitting energy, much like a halo, a white hot manifestation of burning desire. It warmed her body and her heart. Jessica had absolutely no doubt that she had grasped the truth of her *Well of Being*, and that she had just expressed her true life's purpose.

Jessica opened her eyes, blinking in the face of a blazing sun, and when her eyes adjusted to the brightness, she noticed that the well had disappeared from view. She refilled her lemonade glass with the sunny concoction in the pitcher and then settled deeper into the rocker, slowly swaying back and forth as she sipped her drink. Totally relaxed and supremely peaceful, Jessica reached her free hand up to encircle the butterfly pendant hanging from her neck, and she asked it if there was anything else she needed to know about the 5th Chakra. The answer that rang in her ears was, "The Butterfly will tell you." Jessica was a little confused at this response, because she was holding the butterfly, but as she looked down at the pendant in her hand, she saw the blue butterfly from her dream poised on the rim of her glass.

"I'm here to tell you about your Angels, Guides, and Teachers," the butterfly said.

And Jessica replied back with a chuckle, "I'm all ears!"

The butterfly went on to explain to Jessica that her *Well of Being* was not only the domain of her higher *Self*, but also a resource where a pool of knowledgeable Angels, Guides, and Teachers were at her disposal—ready to assist her when she called upon them. "For instance," the butterfly said, "do you know how to go about fulfilling your life's purpose?"

"No," Jessica said, "I just *know* that it's what I am going to do when I return home."

"Very good," said the butterfly. "I can hear the conviction in your voice. You have set an intention. Let's start with Guides and Teachers first," the butterfly suggested. Jessica's little blue buddy taught her about the differences between nonphysical Guides and Teachers. What she learned was that Guides can be thought of as highly experienced and knowledgeable consultants or mentors who are called upon to assist with specific tasks. In Jessica's case, a Guide could help her with the mechanics of setting up her clothing design business. Nonphysical Teachers deal more with the spiritual advancement of the soul, assisting with the expansion and ever-increasing awareness of the higher *Self* and facilitating one's evolution to higher frequency energy.

Listening intently, a furrow began to form on Jessica's brow and she blurted out, "But how do I know who to talk to and how to talk to them?" Jessica asked.

"One way you communicate with these nonphysical beings is through your feelings," the butterfly went on to explain. "That is why it was so important for you to break through your emotional blocks and to shed your outer shell. It was crucial for you to balance your 2nd Chakra, the orange frequency, before you began your ascension to the higher Chakras. Communication with your Guides and Teachers often occurs through the use of symbols. These symbols may take the form of synchronistic events, coincidences, flashes of insight, or intuitive knowings, and they can appear to be insignificant or curious hieroglyphics to the unaware, but they are actually key, very important messages to the open, receptive, and awakened individual. It is your feelings (does something feel good or does it feel bad?) that help you determine whether or not something is a right action or correct forward motion for you."

The butterfly paused and repositioned its feet on the rim of her glass, and Jessica said, "I didn't realize how much opening up my emotions would open up my life. And I never even dreamed I could communicate with non-physical beings. It sounds like something you would see in a science fiction movie!"

"It is so easy to begin the process of connecting with your Guides and Teachers – all you need to do is simply ask. Ask for help using specific questions and intentions. You'll find that whatever you need (be it the perfect person, event, book, seminar, circumstance, or bit of knowledge) will be revealed or will come to you. But you must be willing to follow this guidance with faith and trust, and only if it *feels* right to you."

"That's going to take a little practice for me. But trusting my emotions instead of squashing them is an exciting, new prospect now." Jessica confided.

"Let's move on to the angelic realm."

The butterfly taught Jessica that Angels are highly evolved "beings of consciousness" who are helping to raise awareness on a planetary level. They are pure, joyous, and loving energy. While you do not necessarily have to believe in angels to benefit from their love and encouragement, a good way to access what they have to offer is to pretend that you do. The butterfly suggested that Jessica imagine herself as the crystal vase in her bathroom, and to see herself as ready, willing, and open to being filled with tiny buds or fully expanded blooms of angelic help.

"As with your Guides and Teachers," her little coach continued, "the lines of communication are opened wide when you ask for assistance, and angelic guidance will also come in unexplained knowings, words that pop into your head as if they are being whispered in your ear, visions, colors, or signs. Angels are particularly attentive when you are walking the path of your purpose on this earth, because as you raise *your* consciousness, the consciousness of the entire planet expands and evolves, as well."

"Just knowing angles are watching over me makes me feel special—loved and supported. I know I will need a lot of help when I go back home, but now I realize that all I have to do is ask when I need it." Jessica gratefully said.

The butterfly extended its wings and skipped over to the opposite rim of the glass, closer to Jessica. Its wide round eyes stared intently at her, and as it began to speak, it waved its antennae emphasizing its words. "When you 'go back home', be especially aware of how you use your words. Spoken words have a power all their own, and you can take advantage of that by only expressing what you do want instead of what you do not want. Affirm what you want often, and when you do, speak with emotion, speak with your heart. Singing your affirmations is a fun way to experiment with your voice and your words, too."

"Also, be aware of how you communicate with your fellow humans. Your words can uplift and inspire others or degrade and beat them down. It never bodes well for you when you choose the latter. Remember the woman in your lobby whom you purposely unsettled?"

Still ashamed and embarrassed, Jessica nodded her affirmative answer.

"That bit of banter cost you your job, but even more important, it is not consistent with who you are and the path you have now chosen," continued the butterfly. "So, please, be attentive to how you exchange words with others. Let truth lead the way when you speak. Let the truth ringing in your *Well of Being* be so true that the echo that comes back is always an exact match, with no 'ifs,' 'ands' or 'buts' trailing behind."

"And remember, an exchange means that more than one person is involved. Really listen to others as they talk, and you will be able to hear the truth ringing, or not ringing, in their voices, too. People will call you 'psychic' in your ability to perceive the truth of a matter, but a more apt term would be 'enlightened.'"

Just then Jessica noticed that daylight had faded to dusk. When she commented on it, the butterfly said, "You always have access to the light, whether you see it or not. You can choose to live from your higher *Self*, to rely on your intuition to guide you through your days, or you can stay just as you were when you came to this place. Really, it is a choice between gliding through life with grace and ease or pushing and shoving in struggle. But I see you are weary. This is a discussion for another day. It is time for us to return." And as the words were spoken, Jessica found herself in her rocking chair back on the farm front porch. She did not even have to turn around and look to see that the bathroom door was now visible behind her. She felt it. She knew it was there.

After lingering a while longer in the sublime comfort of the arms of the rocking chair, Jessica slowly stood up, turned around, and reached for the bathroom door knob. Before entering the room, Jessica looked back at the farm porch scene and snapped a shot of it in her mind, including the sights, the sounds, the smells, and the sensations—for she knew this was a place to which she would surely want to return.

On the bed an evening tray was already waiting for her. As Jessica walked closer, she was grateful to see her Chakramid Journal right beside it. Jessica realized she was very tired, so she slipped off her dress and undergarments and hung them on the mirror, put on her nightshirt, and climbed into her cozy, welcoming bed. Turning her attention to her evening meal, Jessica saw that the tray offered a big, leafy tossed salad studded with finely chopped vegetables and tiny cubes of cheese. A fruity ring of sliced apples, pears, and peaches formed a circle around it. The scent of peppermint drifted up to her nose from the reconstructed white teacup she had dropped in shock that morning, and she took a long, heartwarming sip of tea before digging into her salad. When she finished eating, Jessica pushed the tray off to her side with one hand as she sipped more tea from the paper thin white cup. Still sipping, she leaned over and retrieved her journal and laid it on her lap as she sank back into the comfort of the rosy headboard.

Jessica opened her journal and read the 5th Chakra introduction. Then in the book, between thoughtful pauses and peppermint sips, Jessica wrote her first, very own affirmation. Delighted with the endeavor, she held it up, admiring its perfection, as happy as a mother who had just birthed a baby, joyously counting ten fingers and ten toes. Jessica read her affirmation out loud, feeling its power and passion as the words resonated from her lips. Then she put her pen back to work answering questions and recording truths she had learned that day.

Jessica was glad when the journal would allow her to go no further, and she slid under the sheets for a good night's rest. In her dreams, Jessica ran barefoot though a field of wildflowers abounding with butterflies of all shapes, sizes and colors flitting here and there, or pausing to collect nectar from the blooms. As she ran, Jessica was washed in sunlight, with her hair in flight behind her. From time to time she was joined by kind Guides and Teachers, who told her they would be happy to assist her on her journey, and she expressed her sincere thanks and gratitude to them in return.

A large indigo butterfly floating on a cloud of radiating golden light captured Jessica's attention. In her dream, she stopped to behold this vision of captivating beauty. As she examined the butterfly, she realized that the golden light was actually a thick mane of shining, wavy hair. Jessica was startled when a stunning, shimmering, feminine face suddenly lifted up and smiled at her. The beautiful woman said, "You should stop thinking so much." Then she reached out with one shimmery hand and lightly touched Jessica on the forehead right above and between her eyes and said, "Lighten up!" and Jessica awoke. The dream was so real that Jessica could still feel the loving, warm energy that flowed from the woman's hand as it made contact with her forehead. She lay in bed for a while enjoying the sensation, and then she decided to begin her new day.

Jessica stretched her whole body outwards and as she did so she mentally made note of every part and thanked it for serving her in perfect health. Releasing the stretch, she sat up swinging her legs over the edge of the mattress. When Jessica stood up, she gave her feet a little stamp and gently rolled her neck in wide, smooth circles. Then Jessica turned her attention to making the bed. She had come to realize that this small task was a daily opportunity for her to practice being in the present moment as she pulled, straightened, tucked, and smoothed. When she was finished, she gathered up her freshly laundered and pressed dress and undergarments and headed to the bathroom.

The door knob appeared as expected and once inside, Jessica hung her clothing on the hook on the back of the door. Glancing at the vanity, Jessica was delighted to see the crystal vase overflowing with a big bouquet of blue hydrangeas. The puffy blue cloud of flowers floated over the clear container in a spectacular display. Jessica entered the shower and stood in the steamy waterfall for quite a while before she lathered up with the chamomile shower gel she found there. Its scent was subtle but refreshing. Jessica exited the shower in a peaceful, relaxed state, although she felt an underpinning of anticipation as she readied herself for the day and for a new round of learning and insight. After she was dressed, Jessica opened the bathroom door. As she did, she heard the elevator call to her with the ding of its bell and the swishing sound of the doors sliding open.

Calmly crossing the room, Jessica entered the second elevator. Scrutinizing the Second Power Pack, she could see that the first disk, the blue one, was rotating at the same rhythmic pace as the disks in the First Power Pack on the elevator next to her. Jessica reached up and pushed the second button, which was of the same indigo hue as the butterfly in her dream last night. During her ascent, Jessica wondered what the gallery wall would say to her today. But when she exited the elevator, Jessica did not even notice the new painting hanging in the middle of the third row. She did not notice the new indigo stripe above it. And she did not notice her dress as it turned from sky blue to indigo. What she did see was someone sitting in her chair in the middle of the room. At long last, Jessica was no longer alone.

6th Chakra

"I see"

Even though she remained seated facing the gallery wall with her hands loosely folded in her lap, Jessica immediately recognized her visitor as the luminous lady from her dream. Jessica was so shocked at seeing the motionless form that she hesitated, wondering what she should do. She could get right back on the elevator and try to return to where she had come, or she could move forward and see what she could learn. Jessica chose to continue her journey, and she resolutely walked over to the Being in her chair. Still staring straight ahead, the woman said, "Have you seen your new painting on the wall?"

It was hard for Jessica to tear her eyes away from the stranger, but she turned and faced the gallery wall and focused on its new message. Positioned to the right and in perfect formation with the blue painting, the new canvas revealed the words, "I see" in indigo paint.

Jessica said, "Yes, it says 'I see.'"

The lady responded, "Yes, you see me. Before, it was easier for you to believe your butterfly necklace was communicating with you than to consider that you are your own source of knowledge and wisdom. But after you dipped deep into your *Well of Being*, after you opened yourself to the truth, you can now see me. I am your inner, higher *Self*."

Jessica was taken aback for a moment and then she blurted out, "But you are so beautiful."

"As you are."

"But you are the perfect size, the perfect shape—the perfect everything," Jessica continued.

"As you are. You can choose to change your outer appearance if you like. That is what your free will is for. But what I want you to understand is that you are perfect now, just as you are. And if you choose to change, I implore you to see the perfection in the process and to love and accept yourself as perfect every step of the way."

"Why haven't I seen you before?" Jessica asked.

"Do you remember what I told you in your dream last night?"

"Yes, you told me to lighten up. That really was you?" asked Jessica.

"Yes," *Self* replied. "Often it is impossible for you to hear or see your *Self* because of all the thoughts and images spinning around in your head. However, when your conscious mind is closed or busy, *Self* can communicate with you in your dreams. The quandary is that sometimes you remember your dreams when you awake and sometimes you do not. And oftentimes the message does not seem clear to you even if you do remember. Last night it was much easier to reach your subconscious mind, because you were so open."

"Yes," Jessica affirmed, "I did remember my dream last night. In fact, it was so real that I actually felt your touch even after I woke up. But what did you mean when you said 'Lighten up?'"

"Remember how your mind was racing, how your thoughts were running together when you first came to this place?" asked *Self.*

"Yes," said Jessica. "I was always thinking anxious, fearful thoughts and I used my anger to mask the bad feelings they created."

"Well, when you 'lighten up,' you open up. By ridding your mind of the useless garble you are used to generating, by cleaning things up in there, you can see and hear the truth."

"How do I do that?" Jessica wanted to know.

"Actually, you practiced one way this morning as you made your bed. Dwelling in the present moment and being mindful of what you are doing is a great start. Many people naturally do that while performing household chores, gardening, walking, running, or playing with children. Meditation is really the best way, though..."

Jessica cut her *Self* off just as final as slamming a door in her face saying, "I tried that and I just could not keep my mind quiet. Meditation doesn't work for me."

"I see," said *Self*.

Jessica felt an awkward pause in the conversation and she waited for *Self* to continue, but she did not. Jessica's attention was suddenly diverted by the bathroom door as it faded into view. When she looked back to *Self* to express her surprise at the door's appearance without being summoned, she found the chair empty, and *Self* nowhere to be seen. Jessica walked over to the door and put her hand on the door knob, and then she twisted her torso around to see if *Self* had reappeared. Since she had not, Jessica turned the knob and tried to push the door open, but it would not budge. Something told Jessica to open the door towards her and when she did, Jessica was facing a wall of water. As she peered inside, she realized that what she was seeing was the inside of an aquarium she and Michelle had owned as children. Jessica recognized the shocking pink gravel, the fake plants swaying in the circulating water and, of course, the plastic diver poised by his ever opening and closing plastic treasure chest. The familiarity of the scene drew Jessica in and she walked through the watery threshold unaware of the door fading away behind her. Jessica held her breath and floated in the aquarium, delighting in its life size.

When she needed to take a breath, Jessica turned around and thought of the bathroom door, but it did not appear at her command. Jessica thrashed her arms about in what she thought was the general vicinity of the door, but she could feel nothing. Panic overtook Jessica and her frantic mind churned with thoughts of fear and terror. *Why did I come in here? Am I going to die? What am I going to do? Where is Self?* Suddenly, seemingly out of nowhere,

Self appeared to Jessica and told her to breathe. Jessica shook her head no, for surely she would suck water into her lungs and die. *Self* said, "Ordinary rules do not apply in this place—Breathe!" Jessica gasped as she took a deep breath, drawing air into her lungs. After a few more gulps, Jessica started to calm down.

Self took Jessica by the hand and guided her to the treasure chest at the bottom of the tank and motioned for her to sit down. Jessica sat on top of the chest with her feet firmly grounded in the gravel. Resting in her lap, palms up, her hands were loosely open and relaxed. *Self* took the diver's place by her side supporting and comforting Jessica. Then she whispered instructions in Jessica's ear, telling her to draw in a deep, even breath and as she exhaled, to watch the bubbles flowing from her lips. Jessica did as *Self* advised, and she relaxed even more as she observed each bubbly round pass her lips and float from view.

Then *Self* suggested that Jessica take any thoughts she was thinking, and without any admonishments or judgment, encapsulate them in a bubble and watch them float from view, too. As Jessica tried this technique, she was fascinated by the proliferation and content of her thought bubbles. "I wonder what is going to happen next?" was one. "Is this really meditation?" was another. "Am I doing this right?" and on and on. But after a while Jessica noticed the thought bubbles were coming farther and farther apart and immediately popping instead of floating in her awareness for so long.

Just then Jessica knew it was the void between her thoughts (the pauses, the gaps, or the domain of "no thought") where real meditation took place. She also knew, however, that thoughts bubbling up from the silence were a natural part of the process, and she should not consider them proof that she could not meditate, nor should she interpret them as a sign that she was not doing it right. Jessica was content with this knowing and she was thoroughly enjoying the physical manifestations—the lightness and peacefulness—of her meditation.

Jessica knew it was her *Self* who was imparting these knowings to her. And as she turned to look at her, *Self* said, "When you meditate, it is just like you are sitting on a treasure chest, an endless source of wisdom and knowledge. This wealth of information is yours for the taking. It is your inheritance from Infinite Intelligence."

The peacefulness Jessica was embracing was momentarily interrupted by an explosive POP, immediately followed by a loud sucking sound. Jessica found herself in the middle of a mini-tornado, with water swirling round and round her. She could see that the water level was receding, and she watched without moving for quite a while as all of the water gradually drained from the tank. And as the water disappeared from view, so did the plants and the gravel. Jessica was still seated on the treasure chest though—her access to collective consciousness.

Looking all around, Jessica noticed she was once again in an all-white room, a tiny replica of the space she had entered when she stepped off of the elevator for the first time. The same, that is, with two notable exceptions. There was no red stripe encircling the room, and there were two doors now, the one that led into the bathroom and another one visible directly across from it. This second door was an exact duplicate of the first one, right down to the gleaming white door knob. It did have what appeared to be raised white letters on it, though, and Jessica left her seat to see what they said. Standing before the door Jessica read, "i i i Conference Room." Jessica fleetingly wondered why the third "i" was underlined. *What did the third "i" mean?* Looking over her shoulder at the door leading back to the safety and familiarity of her striped room, Jessica chose to go on. However, even in her meditative state, Jessica's humor emerged as she lightheartedly said, "I choose what's behind Door #2," and she turned the knob and opened the door.

This door opened into a formal conference room. Rich, walnut wood panels rising half way up the walls warmed the white painted room. The only furniture in it was a huge, heavy, walnut conference table where 17 people were seated—eight along each long edge and one at the foot of the table. The "power seat" at the head of the table was beautifully appointed with gently curved arms and intricately carved details. As Jessica stood frozen in the doorway, she wondered where *Self* was and what she should do. *Self* was seated at the foot of the conference table and when Jessica thought of her, she rose up and went over to Jessica. Taking her by the hand, *Self* led Jessica to the head of the table and invited her to sit down. Jessica did so and from this vantage point she could clearly see each of the seated individuals. When no one said anything after a while, Jessica shifted uncomfortably in her seat, wondering why everyone was staring back at her and no one was speaking.

Self explained to Jessica that this was a very special place to which she always had access. She continued by explaining this was the domicile of her Third Eye, which was located on her forehead, slightly above and between her eyes. (Now, Jessica realized the significance of the underlined letter "i" in the door's signage. It wasn't an acronym; it was a symbol for her Third Eye!) Here she had access to her personal council of Angels, Guides, and Teachers. While she had already been introduced to them in her 5th Chakra experience, that had been for the purpose of excavating her truth, and ultimately her purpose.

On the farm she had discovered the seeds of her truth that were ready to be planted, cultivated, and nurtured. Now she could take that truth and access the power of her i i i Council for gaining insight, using her intuition, and activating her imagination to create her vision, the bigger picture of her life's purpose. However, while these Beings were always available to her, they would only offer advice, help, or assistance if she asked them for it. They each had their own specialty, but their purpose was solely to support her in her endeavors, not to independently influence her in any way.

Jessica's attention was particularly drawn to a beautiful woman dressed in a lovely, white, silky dress. The woman's face softly shone as bright as the lustrous fabric clothing her. Addressing the woman, Jessica asked her about her specialty. The woman stood up and visibly brightened as she started to speak. She told Jessica that she was a dressmaker and that she watched over Jessica as she worked on her clothing creations. She added how filled with joy she became when Jessica expressed her desire to design clothes to help people understand and balance their own Chakras, and that she would help Jessica in any way that was asked to assist in that endeavor. Then the woman said no more. She took her seat and continued to smile lovingly at Jessica. Jessica's body felt warm all over and when she looked down at her hands, she saw a soft, subtle light radiating from them that she knew was energy. She wondered if this was also part of what *Self* meant when she said, "Lighten up." Still at Jessica's side, *Self* confirmed this was so. She explained that when Jessica accessed the loving guidance of her **i i i** Council and her higher *Self*, she was *living in the energy of the light.*

"Remember on the farm when I told you that you never have to dwell in darkness?" asked *Self.*

"Yes, I do."

"This is what I meant," said *Self.* "You have the freedom of choice to live in the light, to work with the tools of insight, intuition, and imagination...or not."

"How do I do that?"

"You have already learned several different ways to communicate with your *Self* and your **i i i** Council. One is through your emotions—by asking, "Does this feel good or does this feel bad?"—and paying attention to how you feel. Other ways include staying in the present moment and meditation. One more powerful, extremely effective tool is visualization. Visualization is a process that allows you to 'see' the end result of what you wish to be, do, or have, and it can offer the means for attaining that end."

"Can I try it now?" Jessica asked.

"Certainly," said *Self.* "Actually, getting in a meditative, completely relaxed state before visualizing greatly enhances its effectiveness. I will take my place at the table and guide you through it."

Self returned to her seat at the end of the table. As she sat down, a light shone on the wall directly behind and slightly above her, similar to the one projected in Jessica's striped room when she reviewed videos from her past for the first four Chakras. Jessica suddenly realized it was her *Self* who controlled the images she viewed then, just as it was now. *Self* invited Jessica to relax her body and to look at the screen projected outside of her. As Jessica did so, she noted that all of her Angels, Guides, and Teachers were also within view, and she was seeing through the eyes of *Self*, strategically positioned in front of the projection. With the help of her **i i i** Council, Jessica began to see herself in a completely different light. Her thoughts were putty in her hands as she patted, rolled, kneaded, shaped, and smoothed them out into the life of her dreams.

Jessica started with her apartment. She envisioned a little bit larger space nestled in an exciting, growing part of town, and it was the tranquil and inspiring haven she had always wanted her home to be. She imagined herself driving a cute, sporty, little, fuel-efficient car. She pictured herself gliding though the doors of her very own company, located in a chic ware-house with plenty of room for her to create, store, and distribute her designer line of Chakramid clothing and inspirational items. She saw herself in loving, healthy relationships with family and friends, and there was even a romantic interest in her life!

At the end of her visualization, Jessica asked her **i i i** Council for a plan of action for making her vision her reality. Several ideas immediately came to her mind for initial steps to take, and Jessica was content with that, knowing she would be divinely guided and supported every step of the way. All she had to do was remember to ask, be attentive to the information, the signs, and the synchronicities presented to her, and then take inspired action with faith and gratitude. Jessica warmly and graciously thanked her entire council for their help as she rose from her seat at the head of the table. She felt absolutely wonderful. It was as if she was floating in a sea of light, love, and inspiration, and as she turned to leave, she felt buoyant, joyful, and complete. When she thought of it, the door appeared, and with one last smile and nod of appreciation to her council, Jessica turned the door knob and entered her bathroom.

The gleaming white bathroom was a welcome relief (for the obvious reason). As Jessica washed her hands in the sink, she admired her new flow-ery friends that filled the crystal vase. A bunch of Queen Anne's Lace made a light, airy, and open arrangement. Jessica thought it was certainly a perfect metaphor for the wonderful way she felt right now. As she looked closer to admire the blooms, Jessica noticed a single dot of indigo at the heart of each frilly head, and she imagined that she was the indigo dot floating in a field of infinite possibilities. Jessica laughed at the notion that this extraordinary flower that held such meaning for her was usually considered an obnoxious weed.

Looking beyond the flowers, Jessica caught a glimpse of herself in the mirror. While Jessica usually took a quick peek to see if she looked okay or if her makeup needed touched up or her hair needed combed, this time her quick look turned into quite a stare. Jessica wondered if she could actually see the colors associated with her Chakras reflecting from her body somehow. She had heard of people seeing "auras," whatever that meant. If a person's aura was an outward reflection of their Chakras, though, was it possible she could she see her own?

Jessica stepped back from the mirror until she could see her entire body in the reflection. Then she looked intently at her feet, legs, and hips. Could she see any colors emitting from them? No, Jessica acknowledged, she could not. If she could see the colors, though, what would she see? Using her imagination, Jessica flooded those areas of her body with red light. Moving up slightly to the area of her stomach below her belly button, she made a quick scan, and seeing nothing, mentally filled that area with orange light. She continued on just above her navel. That area was surveyed and then splashed with yellow light. Jessica lovingly looked at her chest and then she extended her arms out with her palms up. She then gave her heart, arms and hands a broad sweep of green light. Jessica's throat area received a look and was then promptly painted blue. Finally, Jessica focused on her eyes, her brows, and her forehead, after which she colored them deep reddish blue. As Jessica looked at her multi-colored self, her body felt put together, in sync, and balanced. She stood facing the mirror a while, soaking up this enjoyable sensation before her thoughts turned to her Chakramid Journal. Jessica was ready to journal the day's lessons and to record her life's vision. And as the door appeared, Jessica stepped into her vibrant, multi-striped room.

Jessica's eyes took in all of the colors on the walls as she entered her amazing room, and she couldn't resist an urge to twirl round and round in the middle of it. As she spun, the colors swirled together in a rich, bright blur. When Jessica stopped, she felt delightfully dizzy, like a child who had just experienced her first amusement park ride. Walking over to her rosy bed, Jessica picked up her Chakramid Journal and opened it to the 6th Chakra Chapter. She thoughtfully leafed through the introduction, and then she looked at the evening tray that had been sitting beside her book. The tray offered a bounty of blue and purple berries and red and purple grapes. Whole wheat crackers and a nice selection of sliced meat and cheeses rounded out the meal. Jessica slid the tray to the head of the bed, sat down, and popped a grape into her mouth. It was juicy, tangy, and delicious. Jessica slowly savored her meal as she mindfully ate. When she was full, she pushed the tray aside and sipped on a glass of grape juice that appeared in its place.

Jessica picked up her journal and found a comfortable position leaning against her voluptuous, padded headboard. There were a few questions to answer after the 6th Chakra introduction, followed by a generous number of blank pages that were literally begging Jessica to document what she had learned and to paint a written picture of her newly created life's vision. As she recorded her visualization, paying special attention to the part laying out a plan of action, Jessica realized she was adding some new details that she had not been provided before, and she noted that writing in her journal was another tool for the Third Eye, because as she wrote and invited inspiration, it was as if her pen was being guided by her *Self* and her i i i team.

Jessica sank even deeper into the headboard and leaned her head back and closed her eyes. As she did so, she saw a formula, a Third-Eye equation, which she knew she had to share with the world. With her eyes still closed, Jessica wrote IA= i + i + i in her Chakramid Journal. Just as Einstein had formulated his famous Relativity equation after visualizing a ride on a beam of light, so did Jessica conceive her i i i recipe for living an enlightened life, as she mentally revisited the day's light trip in her mind. The three "i's" stood for Imagination plus Insight plus Intuition and "IA" represented the result, which was Inspired Action. By living in the light, by seeing through the eyes of *Self,* and with the assistance of her i i i Council, Jessica knew that struggle and hardship could be a thing of the past. Continuing to draw on her insight,

Jessica also knew that our stay here on Earth was meant to be happy, prosperous, and joyful, and that anything less meant we were dwelling in a dim, shadowy, or dark state of mind of our own making.

Jessica was suddenly extremely tired, and she briefly thought of allowing herself to drift to sleep while leaning up against her headboard. But she did not want to rumple her dress, so in her semiconscious state, she left the bed, stripped off her dress and underclothes, and hung them on the hanger suspended from the mirror. Not bothering to put on her nightshirt, Jessica slowly climbed back into bed and slipped her bare body beneath the sheets. The light in the room grew dimmer and dimmer, until it was completely dark by the time Jessica's head fell softly on the pillow, and she was soon fast asleep.

In her dreams Jessica rode on a light beam with Einstein. Unlike the twirling amusement park ride she had experienced during the day, they were on a roller coaster now going at the speed of light, zipping through the galaxy and passing innumerable planets and stars. At the end of the ride Einstein turned to Jessica with his wild white hair glowing against the backdrop of space, and he told her she had dipped into the same source to create her Inspired Action formula that he had accessed when he wrote his Theory of Relativity—and that source was Infinite Intelligence. Then with a quick wink, Einstein was gone. Jessica was momentarily alone before a huge white moth flew up. It hovered in front of her and said, "You are God." Hearing those blasphemous words, Jessica abruptly woke up.

Lying in bed, Jessica chuckled to herself when she imagined how her grandmother would react if someone told *her* that *she* was God. A guarantee of fire and brimstone would certainly erupt from her mouth, mixed with the hatred she automatically employed when encountering anything foreign to her. It definitely would not be a pretty sight. Casting those thoughts aside, Jessica mentally prepared herself for the coming day, which she suspected would be her last in this space. She enjoyed a good morning stretch and then slowly and purposely rolled out of bed onto her feet. She gave them a little stomp, and then Jessica focused on making up her bed. During the task, Jessica purposefully did not consider the words spoken by the moth, because she knew their meaning would soon be revealed to her. When she finished, Jessica gathered up her garments and headed to the bathroom door.

As she walked into the bathroom, Jessica peered at the frothy Queen Anne's Lace standing at attention in the lead crystal vase. The vision was just as lovely and meaningful as it had been the day before. Jessica hung up her clothing and entered the shower. After a heavenly rosemary-scented wash, Jessica emerged before the vanity. Stepping back several paces, she scanned her entire body, bathing each part in the appropriately colored light. Jessica felt confident, powerful, and complete. Then she groomed and dressed her body. When she was ready, Jessica purposefully walked out the bathroom door, went over to the second elevator, and entered its open doors for her final ascent.

7th Chakra

"I know"

Jessica pushed the last button next to the violet-colored disk as she noted the blue and indigo spheres spinning in sync. In comparison, their violet counterpart was turning around somewhat slower. Jessica's last trip upward in the elevator was swift and silent. When the car stopped, Jessica exited and immediately walked over to her gallery wall. The third row was now complete; its final canvas, which Jessica already knew said, "I know" in violet lettering, hung in its place on the wall. For the first time she recognized the handwriting on the wall—it was her own! Through the eyes of her *Self*, Jessica had painted and hung each canvas, but back in her unconscious state she could not see them. The signs had been there all along, but it was only as she allowed in the light, and as she opened up to each new level of Chakra energy awareness, that she finally was able to see each of the canvases.

As Jessica stood gazing at her gallery wall, she shifted her attention upward and smiled at the seventh and final stripe. It was a violet band of color that traveled the perimeter of the room, just like the luxurious violet fabric wrapped around Jessica's body. Although it appeared to be half the size of the other stripes, Jessica knew this stripe changed at the halfway point from violet to white, so the top half of it blended in with the remaining white on the walls. She slowly walked to her chair, uncertain of what to do next. Sitting down, Jessica rejected the thought of food and instead ordered up a comforting cup of tea.

The tray appearing at her feet held a steamy pot of water, her white tea cup and saucer, and a variety of aromatic tea bags. Leaning over, Jessica poured hot water into her cup, chose a bag, and submerged it in the little hot tub. Then she straightened up in her chair, leaving the bag to steep for a while. Looking back, Jessica knew the flash of light that had preceded her first meal was just meant to get her attention, and the flashing stopped when she realized she automatically received whatever she was thinking about. Jessica leaned over once again and picked up her elegant white cup, filled to the brim with a spicy-smelling brew. Righting herself in her chair, Jessica silently sipped her tea until the cup was empty.

Returning the cup and saucer to the tray, Jessica stood up and began to stroll around the room. As she did, she picked a color—starting with the red stripe at the floor—and imagined it in the corresponding part of her body, while walking at a moderate, serene pace. Jessica strolled around her abode seven times, absorbing each of the seven colors. Earlier in the morning, she had performed the same exercise in her bathroom before her mirror, but this time, with the addition of the new violet/white stripe, she filled herself with the full rainbow spectrum. When she stopped, Jessica felt blissfully light-footed, lighthearted, lightheaded, and ready for what was to come, so she put her attention on the bathroom door and entered the room.

This was the first time a room had reappeared, and Jessica was very happy to be back in her meditation space. As before, the vanity had been lowered to a kneeling alter height and a river rock fountain was making a lovely, melodic sound where the sink had been. There were still seven large white candles on the alter, and their fiery tongues were wagging in unison at the end of their wicks. Lotus Flower incense sticks sent up smoky swirls that flavored the air, and the crystal vase was filled with lavender and fat white rose buds, adding the perfect finishing touch to the tranquil space. On the floor in the middle of the room, a single, plump, velvet cushion, half violet and half white, awaited Jessica.

Slowly lowering her body to the floor, Jessica sat on the cushion with her knees out to her sides and her ankles crossed close to her body. She took one last appreciative look at the alter before closing her eyes and totally relaxing every inch of her body. Jessica centered her attention on her breath, the way *Self* had taught her. At the thought of *Self*, Jessica wondered why she had not seen her today, and then just as quickly, she knew. In her 5th Chakra experience, Jessica could only <u>hear</u> *Self*; in the 6th Chakra, she could also <u>see</u> *Self*; and now in the 7th Chakra experience, she would be totally integrated with *Self*—she would <u>be</u> *Self*. With this knowledge, Jessica sat up a little straighter, knowing that along her spine were seven spinning, perfectly aligned Chakras. Jessica resumed her breathing meditation technique and soon found herself in a profoundly sublime place.

In this deep, dreamy state, Jessica's attention was drawn to the space opposite the door though which she had entered the bathroom. Here, the new white door once again appeared, but there was no identifying placard on it this time. Jessica stood up, walked over to the door, opened it and started to enter; but suddenly terrified, she thrust out both of her arms on the bathroom side of the threshold, leaving her teetering with one foot in the physical realm and the other poised to enter a black abyss. Turbulent thoughts frantically bubbled from Jessica: *What is in the darkness? How far down does it go? Is there something to support me that I cannot see?* But then Jessica got a hold of her *Self*, and releasing her hold on the threshold, she stepped into the dark unknown, and began to fall.

As Jessica plummeted downward, her violet skirt flew up into the air. Despite her dire straights, Jessica held her skirt down with her hands, and she couldn't help thinking she must look like a famous picture she had once seen of Marilyn Monroe doing the same thing over a grate on a street. Just then, Jessica's descent abruptly ended, and relief flooded over her when she realized she was standing on something solid. Jessica knelt down in the darkness to take a closer look at what had saved her, and when she did, her knees sank into something soft, spongy, and a little fuzzy. Looking from side to side, Jessica could see she was in the middle of two round, black eyes...and they were staring at her! Startled, Jessica fell out of her crouch, landing on her behind with her legs stretched out in front of her. Then from somewhere below the eyes, Jessica heard a soft and kind, "Hello!"

The benevolent tone in the voice instantly calmed Jessica, so she responded, "Hi, there" in return.

The voice continued, "I'm here to give you the tour."

Jessica rearranged her legs into her cross-legged position, and still sitting in between the peering eyes she said, "I know. I've been waiting for this all my life." And with that she started to move forward.

As Jessica checked out her surroundings, she realized the space into which she had fallen was not entirely dark as she initially had thought, and the reason she could see anything at all was because of the softly glowing lights all around her. As a matter of fact, when she put her attention on them, she could see that the entire space was studded with twinkling white lights. Some were single, some were in clusters, and some had pulled together so tightly that they created large, cohesive masses. Jessica looked behind her and confirmed she was indeed riding on the head of a huge white moth, just like the one that had appeared in her dream the night before. Its massive wings were motionless now as they soared along, and she could see they had subtle tan markings with violet-tinged pointy tips.

Jessica's great moth mentor glided to a stop to start the lesson on the 7th Chakra, the Crown Chakra. "You are in the field of pure consciousness. Here you have full access to the wisdom of the ages. Here you are infinite potentiality. It is the space of absolute awareness on a cosmic level. There are two currents of consciousness running parallel through this space. To help you understand, imagine a crown on your head."

As she thought the thought, Jessica felt something resting on her head. Her hands flew up to confirm what it was and she could feel that a simple, jeweled crown was now adorning her head.

The moth continued with its message. "The band of the crown represents the first current. This is where the physical meets the infinite for the purpose of manifestation or creation in your world. All physical creation is first a thought, so it is easy to see that manifestation would begin in the 7th Chakra. That thought then descends to the 1st Chakra. The seed is deposited in fertile ground, so to speak, and blooms into physical manifestation. How quickly something manifests depends upon the alignment of all of the Chakras; in other words, how balanced the thinker is. Very often the growth (and therefore the fruition) of a manifesting thought is stuck in one level or another until it can break through that area and continue its expansion to manifestation. Here is where a clear 2nd Chakra becomes key. Because emotion speeds up the manifesting process of bringing thoughts into being, feelings can literally propel a thought through the Chakra system into reality. But this is where it gets sticky. You have to be sure that what you are consistently thinking about is what you want to create. Thoughts are powerful things; think them with care."

Jessica was fascinated with what the moth was telling her, but her focus was suddenly diverted to a point of light just ahead that was wildly blinking like a beacon in their direction. "I hate to interrupt," she said, "but I think someone or something is trying to get our attention."

"Let's take a closer look," said the moth.

As they glided toward the light, Jessica could now see it was not a pinpoint of light at all, but a glowing white butterfly, and what she thought was blinking was the flapping of its wings. But even though its wings were moving, the butterfly remained in a stationary position.

"Now," said the moth, "look very closely and tell me what you see."

As Jessica stared intently at the white butterfly, she could see that at its core was a woman sitting alone in a cafe. Jessica told her mentor what she saw and the moth said, "The butterfly is a facilitator for the transformation taking place in its human subject. If you touch my antennae, you can hear her thoughts through the antennae of her butterfly helper. It's like tuning in a radio really."

Jessica untangled her legs and in a kneeling position, reached out her right hand as far as she could, and touched the moth's antennae. As soon as her fingertips met the receiver, she suddenly found herself in the busy cafe, seated across from the woman she had seen through the white butterfly. Judging from the fact that the woman had not reacted to her sudden appearance, Jessica assumed she could not been seen.

Surveying her new surroundings, Jessica noticed there was a half eaten sandwich and cup of coffee pushed off to the side of the table, and the woman was totally absorbed in the task of scribbling in a notebook laid out before her. Jessica could hear her voice, but the woman's lips were not moving. "I am so tired of my life right now. I want to change everything…including me. I want to make a difference, to put my stamp on the world, to help others. I want to meet new people, especially those who share my passion for living a meaningful life, not just droning along purposelessly doing the same thing day after day. I have devoted my life to studying the Chakras for two years now. My head is ready to explode with all of the knowledge I have gained, because it needs to be shared. I want to live in the light and teach my knowledge of the Chakras in a big way. I could rent a studio and give classes, but that doesn't feel right to me. I know I am meant to do something bigger. But I don't know what that looks like."

As Jessica sat across from the woman, she instantly recognized the business partner she had written about in her Chakramid Journal. Jessica had scribbled just as passionately in her journal as the woman before her was doing now, about meeting someone who could complement the design business she had planned out in her thoughts. Someone who could fortify her knowledge about the Chakras and integrate those knowings into the clothing line Jessica wanted to create. The woman's eyes were wet with tears that sprang from a well of desire being stymied by frustration. As she quickly blinked the tears away, one escaped from her lashes and slowly began to slide down the apple of her cheek. Jessica longed to wipe it away and to tell her she was not alone. And as she thought the thought, the woman sat up a little straighter in her chair and wrote in her journal, "I know I am not alone. I know there is someone out there who shares my desires and we will find each other, and together we will fulfill our destiny." A warm, encouraged smile spread across the woman's lips, and as she began to gather up her things, Jessica found herself once again sitting on the back of the Great White.

"Wait a minute," Jessica pleaded. "I need to know her name. I must know how I can get in touch with her."

The moth said in a calm, reassuring voice, "Your intuition will be your guide to her. Just follow the signs that will show you the way. You will find you are more sensitive now, and you will resonate with many others who share your quest. If you look out over the field of consciousness, you will see what I mean."

As Jessica looked out over the boundless, timeless space, the moth continued his lesson. "The woman's 'Transformator' appeared to be calling your attention to it because you were resonating on the same vibration as the woman. Just look and you can see the clusters of beings that have gravitated to each other for a common purpose, or simply because they share the same vibration frequency. The larger masses are a multitude of clusters that have been attracted together. These are powerful vortexes that can literally raise the consciousness of the planet."

As the moth paused, Jessica asked, "What are...did you call them 'Transformators'?"

The moth answered, "Yes. Transformators are pure, loving energy that help humans during their transformative process. They serve their subjects by assisting them in "mating," or in other words, matching up, or finding others who are like-minded. A Transformator's sole purpose is to bring together people who are resonating similarly in transforming or changing their lives, thoughts, or actions; and they use synchronistic events, happenings, situations, or things as opportunities to do that. And as you saw with the woman in the cafe, they also serve as a conduit of communication. They facilitate telepathic or physical exchanges of ideas. That is how the woman in the cafe actually received your thoughts when you wanted to comfort her in her despair."

Just as those last words floated up to Jessica from below the moth's piercing black eyes, Jessica noticed another Transformator that drew her attention. She did not even have to say any words this time and the moth started to glide toward it. As they drew closer, Jessica looked hard into its core and was surprised to see one of the executives at her previous job. She hesitated for just a moment before she touched one of the moth's antennae to tap into his thoughts, and as she did so, Jessica found herself back in her former lobby, facing her old receptionist's desk. Of course, Jessica had noticed this guy before. He was friendly and good looking and she often watched him out of the corner of her eye as he passed by her desk on his way to meetings or to lunch. Now he was smiling and nodding at the pretty woman whom Jessica assumed was her replacement. "Why am I here?" Jessica peevishly muttered.

The man brushed his fingers along the desk as he passed and nodded to the woman behind it with a smile. "I wonder what really happened to Jessica," he thought. At this, Jessica's full attention was captured and she continued to listen in. "I can't believe she would purposely sabotage our new advertising consultant. Why would she do that? Maybe she just made a mistake."

"Well, anyway, I will probably never see her again. Too bad though. I always felt there was something different about her, something deeper hiding under that facade. I could see she was desperately trying to fit in by wearing designer fashions like the other women. But they were always too tight and she didn't really look comfortable in them. Sometimes she would come to work in outfits that fit her body—and I'm assuming her personality—like a glove. On those days, she seemed more cheerful and a little more open to people."

"Oh, well, I guess I better make my vacation plans. Greg is hounding me to book my flight to the Caribbean with him. 'We will be princes of the night,' Greg said. 'The ladies will be lining up to meet us.' But I'd really rather use my vacation time to go to that city that has been devastated by flooding. It would feel really good to help someone in need. I could do whatever they ask. I can shovel or push a broom with the best of them. Hmmm, I *can* do that! In fact, I'm going to book my flight there this afternoon! Greg will just have to find someone else to party with."

As he closed the door to her lobby, the man was deaf to the receptionist's cheery, "Hope you have a great weekend, Alan!" and blind to the look of longing to be included that accompanied it. As Alan hurried away from the lobby, Jessica found herself back on the back of her own Transformator.

"If only I had known he thought those things about me..." Jessica said. She had intended to continue, but something inside stopped her in mid-sentence. "But I did know." Those words sprang from Jessica's *Self.* She did know there were many, many times when her eyes met Alan's and instead of being open and receptive to him, she had quickly lowered her eyes to avoid his, or she picked up the telephone pretending to be busy, or she literally turned her back on him and walked the other way.

The moth, who had been staring at Jessica since her return, said, "Yes, you are correct. When your eyes lock with someone else's seemingly by chance, there is usually something deeper going on. It could be you are both vibrating at the same level, which has an attracting force, or there is some kind of message that either or both of you have for the other. But in any event, chance encounters in your world are usually a chance to learn and grow." Although she heard her mentor's words, Jessica's mind had wandered a bit. *Surely the personal items left in my desk are packed up and stored somewhere. Maybe I can use that reason as a means of orchestrating a not-so-chance chance encounter with Alan.* But these musings were interrupted when the moth bellowed below, "Hang on to your crown. We're going up."

Their ascent to the second consciousness current in the 7th Chakra was not a level rise, like her elevator rides. They were traveling at a steep, sharp angle that caused Jessica to hang on to the moth's antennae with one hand and her sliding crown with the other. Jessica knew they were going to the very peak, the pinnacle, the penthouse of the pyramid. When the moth stopped, Jessica repositioned the jostled crown on her head and noticed that the top half of her dress had turned white. Then she stood up to look around. There was a reverent feel to this space, this level of pure consciousness. Unlike the vast number of twinkling lights (or Transformators) in the last level, this infinite space was dotted with only a few, but they were much, much larger, brighter, and more brilliant than the others in the lower level.

The moth spoke up, "The first current of consciousness is oriented toward physical manifestation. It is symbolized by the lower half of your crown, the part that touches the physical—you. The second, higher current is represented by the top half of your crown. It is studded with a few jewels set in a base that is pointed upward, expanding outward toward nonphysical planes. It is oriented to things beyond the physical you; it is a portal to the infinite, the divine, the God in you. Detachment from all things is a requirement for entering this realm, and an empty mind is the vessel that is filled by it. This is the domain of the Christ, the Buddha, Gandhi, Mother Teresa, Einstein, and many others you believe have passed on, but it is also inhabited by many who dwell upon the Earth at this time, of whom you are not aware."

Jessica had been standing, but overcome with wonder and awe; she slowly sank down into a sitting position, and then tucked her legs into her modified lotus pose. She relaxed her body and after one long last look ahead, closed her eyes and cleared her mind. She just sat on the back of the moth without moving and without thinking until she reached a sublime state of bliss. Jessica felt totally unfettered, totally safe, and totally free. There were no limitations on her body and she began to float in the air until she was overlooking the planet Earth. Like a cloud in the sky, Jessica softly blanketed Mother Earth in a warm, harmonious union. She was intimately part of the entire planet and all of its people and all of its things, and they were part of her. Jessica was complete.

Jessica had no idea how long she floated in this eternal, ageless space, but after a while she slowly became aware of her body and her surroundings, and she found herself back in her meditation space, sitting on the violet and white striped cushion on the floor. Jessica continued to sit in the glow of the meditation, not wanting to disconnect her link to her world. When she felt ready, though, Jessica stretched her legs out and then back again as she used her hands to push her body up to stand.

As soon as she stood up, Jessica knew it was "check-out" time. She had done what she had come here to do. She had learned what she had come here to learn. But as she lingered in front of the alter for a few minutes, she noticed that the tight white rose buds had transformed into huge fragrant blooms. Jessica lowered her face into the bouquet and took a deep appreciative breath. Then she carefully pulled a single, perfect stem from the vase and turned to leave. When she arrived at the door, Jessica turned around to take one final look, only to discover that the room had already reverted to a bathroom in the instant her back was to it. She gave the sparkling white, elegant space one last grateful look, and then reached for the white door knob and walked into her rainbow room. The last time she had entered this room, she could not help but spin round and round in its center. But this time as she walked to the middle of the room, *it* was what was spinning now. She stood in the middle of the whirling, colorful vortex and stretched her arms outward from her sides with her palms up—ready, willing, and open.

Jessica knew it was time to gather up her things, so she walked over to her beautiful bed. Standing at its foot, she swept her fingertips over the gorgeous, luxurious bedding, reminiscing about all of the knowledge she had gained journaling and dreaming in its depths. Her suitcase was already packed; all she had to do was zip it up. Looking inside, Jessica saw the few items she had brought with her. But neatly folded beside them were some t-shirts, the kind you receive as a promotional gift. Jessica leafed through the shirts and saw there were seven, each saturated with a Chakra color. They all had the CHAKRAMID label and each was tagged with a card describing the Chakra with which it corresponded. Jessica clapped her hands with glee at this physical manifestation of the new clothing line she intended to create.

Right next to her suitcase was her Chakramid Journal and pen. The pyramid on the cover of the journal was now complete up to its point, which was violet fading to white. Jessica picked up the journal and brought it up to her cheek. She rubbed her face softly against it as she internalized deep gratitude for the book and its contents. Her life was laid out bare in the journal, and then lavishly clothed with dreams, visions, and insights, all woven together with love and faith. She had found the purpose of her life in its pages and had fashioned a pattern for living it there. Jessica lovingly laid the Chakramid Journal on top of the t-shirts and then picked up her pen, which now was filled with a rainbow of seven beads. Her smile deepened as she held the instrument that excavated her soul, and she laid it beside its companion, her journal. Finally, Jessica reverently laid the white rose on top of everything and she zipped up the suitcase and wrapped her fingers around the handle. That was it. It was time to leave. As Jessica slowly walked to the elevator, she took in all of the details of this once empty room. It was now richly furnished with everything she had needed, and beautifully decorated with all of the colors of a rainbow.

At The End,
A New Beginning

Arriving at the elevator—there was only one now—Jessica pushed the down button. At that, the doors glided open, ready to receive her. Jessica stepped only as far as the threshold, and then turned around for what she had thought would be her last look, but with a suggestion from *Self,* Jessica realized she could return to the room any time she wished. With that happy thought, Jessica walked into the middle of the elevator and looked for the Power Pack. Both Power Packs were integrated now—seven through five on the top and four to one on the bottom. All of the disks were spinning in sync, vibrant and balanced. Jessica pushed the button next to the first disk, the red one, and the elevator doors closed for her descent.

As the elevator took her to the foundation of the pyramid, Jessica thought about the journey she had made through the Chakramid: the manifestation principles she had learned and the altered state of consciousness she had achieved in the seventh; the visions she had seen in the sixth; the truth she heard and spoke in the fifth, the love and forgiveness she found in the fourth; the personal power she gained in the third; the emotions she could finally feel in the second; and the grounding she had attained in the first. As she reached the 1st Chakra in her thoughts, the elevator bounced to a gentle stop on the ground floor. The doors she had just walked through were no longer there, but Jessica knew there would be an identical set on the opposite wall. The doors she originally stepped through obediently opened as Jessica turned toward them.

Once again, Jessica walked down the long, narrow hallway on the deep red runner, and she could see the single door at the end through which she could exit the pyramid. When she arrived at the door, still windowless, she stood there for a second collecting her *Self* before continuing on. Jessica opened the door and stood in awe at what she saw. The outside was barren no more. The grounds were beautifully laid out and landscaped. There were people everywhere. Some were strolling in the gardens, some were sitting on benches before tranquil ponds and fountains, and some were enjoying the thrill of riding the rides in an amusement park. There was a huge parking lot now, with signs marking row after row, and Jessica wondered if her car was still there and if she could find it. But as she walked in the direction she felt she should, she did indeed see her car, sitting alone in a space marked "Reserved."

Jessica stood by her car looking back at the pyramid. It was dull and drab no more. Now it was a Chakramid, striped with all of the colors of the rainbow, and she noticed that the upper three levels had a golden glow about them. As she sat her bag down on the pavement next to her car, she couldn't help wondering if in her unconscious state when she arrived at this place, did she just not see what she was seeing now, or had she been here so long that the pyramid had been completed and the casino—or whatever it was—was now opened for guests? *It doesn't matter either way,* Jessica thought as she opened the car door and slid into the driver's seat. She was happy to see the key was waiting in the ignition for her. Jessica leaned outside, picked up her bag, and hoisted it over the steering wheel onto the passenger seat next to her. Before it plopped all the way down though, she glimpsed something lying on the seat. Jessica slid her hand under the suitcase and pulled out her invitation, which she had brought along for directions. She saw that what she had thought was an empty triangle was actually a rainbow filled pyramid. And as she looked at the beautifully written words, she recognized her own handwriting. She was the one who wrote it. She had accepted an invitation from her *Self* to journey here.

Jessica tried the ignition key and her car started right up. She turned the steering wheel in the direction of a sign marked "Exit" and she followed it until she came to a stop sign in front of the main road. There she paused for a moment, appreciating all of the colors before her: the deep red stop sign; the cheerful orange and yellow flowers by the side of the road; the sea of vivid green lawn that surrounded them; the endless, cloudless blue sky; and the indigo and violet decorative grasses that waved their friendly good-byes.

Now Jessica had a choice to make. She could go back to the safety of her old life, the familiar, the known, or she could fearlessly go forward into the uncertainty of the unknown and build a new life for herself. But the way for her to go was obvious; the decision was easy to make. Because now Jessica was seeing her world with Rainbow Eyes.

APPENDICES

Appendix A – 1st Chakra

Appendix B – 2nd Chakra

Appendix C – 3rd Chakra

Appendix D – 4th Chakra

Appendix E – 5th Chakra

Appendix F – 6th Chakra

Appendix G – 7th Chakra

APPENDIX A

1st Chakra
(or Root Chakra)

COLOR: Red

ELEMENT: Earth

LOCATION: Base of Spine

AFFECTED PARTS OF BODY: Adrenal Glands, Back, Blood, Bones, Coccyx (Tailbone), Feet, Immune System, Legs, Joints, Muscles, Rectum

MISSION STATEMENT: I Have

FOOD: Protein (Including Nuts, Legumes, Meat, etc.), Root Vegetables (Such as Beets, Onions, Potatoes, Radishes, etc.)

CRYSTALS/GEMSTONES: Bloodstone, Onyx, Red Garnet, Red Jasper, Smoky Quartz

SCENTS/ESSENTIAL OILS: Bergamot, Cedarwood, Patchouli, Rose Geranium

In our physical state as Earth bound beings governed by the laws of gravity, we are essentially dependent on the ground for support. A healthy 1st Chakra is based on this need to be physically grounded and supported in all areas of our life. Issues of primary importance are our physical survival (food, shelter, sleep, etc.), feelings of safety and security, and a sense of belonging.

So typically, how we are cared for by our immediate family unit or caregivers early on in life and our initial interactions with society as a whole come together to form our foundation.

A person with a balanced 1st Chakra feels safe and secure, protected and trusting. Self-worth, self-confidence, stability, and a quiet strength shine through in a calm, easygoing manner that affirms feelings of belonging in family, work, and community. Physical needs are expected to be met, and they are with grace and ease. A sense of always having enough fosters a willingness to contribute and to share.

Imbalances in our 1st Chakra can show up as "less than" feelings, such as insecurity, anxiety, nervousness, worry, suspicion, self-consciousness, isolation, and greed. And in the process of trying to overcompensate for or underplay these feelings, a person may: overeat or under eat; be over stimulated or lack energy; be careless and sloppy or meticulously neat; be egotistic and domineering or weak in character and passive; or be extravagant and wasteful with money or a money miser.

The important role that the 1st Chakra plays in supporting you cannot be emphasized enough. Imagine the Chakramid with an underdeveloped or overdeveloped base. A small, puny foundation would be perilously unstable, and an over inflated, excessively large foundation would skew the proportion and shape of the rest of the structure on top. Either way results in an unsettling, unnerving feeling at your very core.

APPENDIX B
2nd Chakra
(or Sacral Chakra)

COLOR: Orange

ELEMENT: Water

LOCATION: Lower Abdomen (Below Navel), Genitals, Womb

AFFECTED PARTS OF BODY: Bladder, Hips, Kidney, Sexual Organs

MISSION STATEMENT: I Feel

FOOD: Liquids (Such as, Water, Tea, Juices)

CRYSTALS/GEMSTONES: Carnelian, Coral, Moonstone, Tigereye

SCENTS/ESSENTIAL OILS: Jasmine, Neroli, Orange, Sandalwood

Stepping up to the 2nd Chakra, it's time to move out of the survival mode of the 1st Chakra's focus on your basic physical needs and start having fun feeling sensual and sexy, and engaging your creative self. The 2nd Chakra attends to your desire for interpersonal relationships and invites others into your life to share your passions, sexuality, and creativity.

The 2nd Chakra level primarily focuses on emotional and sexual energies. Balanced emotions promote a sense of self-worth that allows one to accept all the good, including abundance and prosperity, into his or her life.

And balanced sexual energy generates romance and healthy sexual relationships. The craving to create something physical, outside of oneself, develops at this level, and drawing, painting, writing, and music are excellent outlets for this desire.

A balanced 2nd Chakra leads to feelings of wellness, plenty, pleasure, and joy. You can see this exemplified by those who are fully connected and attuned to their physical and emotional centers. They are comfortable with their bodies and their emotions. Sexual and non-sexual relationships are healthy, and they are based on trust and mutual respect. There is a passion for life that is expressed in everything they do.

Imbalances in the 2nd Chakra are characterized by "living in your head," being out of touch with what your body is telling you, and denying yourself pleasure. Anorexia, bulimia, drug and alcohol abuse, and other addictions are attempts to nurture oneself in this kind of emotionally disconnected or detached state. Sexual dysfunctions are also directly related to imbalances in the 2nd Chakra.

An overactive 2nd Chakra can result in lustful, arrogant, or conceited behavior, and an aggressive desire to control others; whereas an underdeveloped 2nd Chakra can manifest as distrust, resentment, fear, apathy, pessimism, and anti-social conduct. It can also show up as continually worrying about what others think and always following the crowd.

The 2nd Chakra is a very important building block in the Chakramid structure. As such, it is perfectly positioned and proportioned right above the root Chakra, which is the foundation or base of the Chakramid. Emotional awareness and connectedness will become more and more important as you ascend up the Chakramid, because emotions are the magnifying glass through which you will examine, study, evaluate (and ultimately communicate with) all of your Chakras.

APPENDIX C
3rd Chakra
(or Solar Plexus Chakra)

COLOR: Yellow

ELEMENT: Fire

LOCATION: Solar Plexus (Above Navel and Below the Sternum)

AFFECTED PARTS OF BODY: Digestive System, Gallbladder, Liver, Pancreas, Spleen

MISSION STATEMENT: I Act

FOOD: Starches, Complex Carbohydrates (Such as, Whole Grains, Beans, etc.)

CRYSTALS/GEMSTONES: Amber, Calcite, Citrine, Jasper, Topaz

SCENTS/ESSENTIAL OILS: Cinnamon, Geranium, Ginger, Juniper, Lemon, Lemon Grass, Peppermint

As we continue to move up the Chakramid, we note that yellow, the color of the 3rd Chakra, is the last of the earth colors in the rainbow spectrum. It is the icing on the cake, so to speak, of the physical you. A well-adjusted 3rd Chakra sustains your commitment to monitoring and fulfilling the needs of the two lower Chakras, but it also generates the will power, determination, and persistence to move on to the higher levels.

In your early years, if your parents or caregivers instilled in you an "I can do it" attitude, your work at this level may be minimal. You are confident, with a strong sense of purpose and/or a mission in life. You take responsibility for your actions and you exercise your personal power in a fair, ethical, and loving way. You are self-directed, self-confident, and self-empowered. If on the other hand, your younger years were filled with negative feedback or a lack of support in an unloving or unsafe environment, your 3rd Chakra may be over inflated or underdeveloped.

An overactive 3rd Chakra may manifest as constant rage, perfectionism, an inordinate need to be in control, or an inability to slow down. You are in the laser lane, you could be a workaholic, and you may be overly domineering in your relationships. You might be plagued with stomach ulcers or excessive weight around your middle.

A deficient 3rd Chakra is reflected as timid behavior, lack of self-confidence, neediness in relationships, fear of being alone, low energy, or chronic tiredness. There may be an addiction to stimulating substances or you may find yourself acting in a subservient manner in your relationships. Digestive problems may also be present in your life.

A strong 3rd Chakra is vital to your success in ascending to the top of the Chakramid. It is the catalyst for all forward moving endeavors. It's the fire in your belly that produces the power in your life.

APPENDIX D

4th Chakra
(or Heart Chakra)

COLOR: Green

ELEMENT: Air

LOCATION: Heart

AFFECTED PARTS OF BODY: Arms, Breasts, Circulatory System, Hands, Heart, Lungs, Shoulders, Wrists

MISSION STATEMENT: I Love

FOOD: Vegetables

CRYSTALS/GEMSTONES: Aventurine, Emerald, Jade, Rose Quartz, Ruby

SCENTS/ESSENTIAL OILS: Pine, Rose, Ylang Ylang

Once the physical needs of your first three Chakras have been addressed, raising yourself to the 4th level is a breeze...literally. This Chakra's corresponding element is air and its main issues are relationships and love—affairs of the heart—where the 4th Chakra resides. Most important, it is the bridge from the physical part of you to your mental and spiritual dimensions. Love and its many expressions (passion, caring, rapport, unity, understanding, and forgiveness) are the means to and the rewards of a clear 4th Chakra.

Ultimately, the objective of an open 4th Chakra is unconditional love. A love so pure that it is not quantified by any restrictions imposed on it, such as your ideals or the way you think others should act or respond to you. So, in addition to your family and friends, the 4th Chakra also makes it possible for you to "love your neighbor (or fellow man) as yourself."

A person graced with a balanced 4th Chakra has a loving presence that is accepting, warm, friendly, gracious, compassionate, and charismatic. Healthy, loving relationships based on a balanced give-and-take dynamic are the benchmark of this Chakra. As such, an ability to gratefully "receive" as well as to give is readily apparent. Self-love is also a tenant of an open 4th Chakra.

Deficiencies in this area surface as feelings of isolation, withdrawal, paranoia, fear of commitment, lack of self-esteem, and/or depression. Heart defenses may manifest as a tendency to "give everything away," to be totally focused on others while depriving oneself, or as addictions (such as to drugs or alcohol), which are used to suppress or deaden feelings from the heart.

A closed or shielded Heart Chakra can stop the ascension to the higher level Chakras right here, so it is easy to see how important it is to open your heart. Unconditional love is the reward and forgiveness is the key.

APPENDIX E
5th Chakra
(or Throat Chakra)

COLOR: Bright Blue or Turquoise

ELEMENT: Ether, Sound

LOCATION: Throat

AFFECTED PARTS OF BODY: Ears, Gums, Jaw, Mouth, Neck, Nose, Teeth, Throat, Thyroid Gland, Tongue, Vocal Cords

MISSION STATEMENT: I Speak

FOOD: Fruits

CRYSTALS/GEMSTONES: Amazonite, Aquamarine, Sodalite, Turquoise

SCENTS/ESSENTIAL OILS: Chamomile, Eucalyptus, Peppermint, Rosemary

Arriving at the 5th Chakra marks the ascension to what has been called the "Golden Triangle." The Golden Triangle encompasses the last three Chakras, and it is the path to spiritual growth. The 5th Chakra is the first in this divine triad. Its elements are ether and sound, and its emphasis is on your truth. It is important to recognize that this Chakra is a conduit between the intellect of the heart and the intellect of the mind; and when it is open, it allows the heart and the head to align and be in sync.

The 5th Chakra has also been called the Throat Chakra, because it resides at the back of your throat. It is the center of communication and self-expression—verbal, but also telepathic. Be sure to understand that "communication" includes not only *your* expression, but also that of others. This is where we "listen to," appreciate, and learn what others have to offer. The 5th Chakra also stimulates creativity, especially in oral, written, and musical forms.

People with a balanced 5th Chakra are truthful to others, as well as to themselves. They take responsibility for their actions, because they say and do what is true for them. Connections and communications with others are clear and harmonious. Creativity is fully expressed and shared. They follow their intuition and are attentive to the synchronicities and signs that are available to them.

An over stimulated 5th Chakra can be identified in those who dominate conversations, speak negatively, yell, or gossip. Habitual lying may also be a problem. An underdeveloped 5th Chakra may be apparent in persons who are unable to express their true opinions, who ultimately say yes to others when they really mean no, and who may be unable or very slow to make decisions.

As you enter the Gold Triangle on your journey through your Chakras, be aware that just as the Chakramid itself is less visible at this level, you, too, are working primarily with your inner, unseen energies. The ego self is being left behind so that you can climb higher and higher.

APPENDIX F
6th Chakra
(or Third Eye Chakra)

COLOR: Indigo or Purple

ELEMENT: Light

LOCATION: Forehead, Between and Above the Eyes

AFFECTED PARTS OF BODY: Eyes, Forehead, Pineal Gland

MISSION STATEMENT: I See

FOOD: None

CRYSTALS/GEMSTONES: Amethyst, Labodorite, Lapis Lazuli, Sodalite, Sugalite

SCENTS/ESSENTIAL OILS: Basil, Juniper, Passionflower, Rosemary

The "i's" have it at the 6th Chakra, or Third Eye, level, because this is where imagination, intuition and insight reign supreme. The psychic tool of Clairvoyance, or clear seeing, also originates in this Chakra.

A clear 6th Chakra is the catalyst that sparks creative genius by uniting the left and right brain hemispheres, thereby merging the intuitive, feeling brain and the rational, thinking brain. And it is where the line between dreams and reality becomes blurred as one embraces the concept that we all have the power to create the life of our dreams.

Your self image (or imagined self) is developed and perpetuated (and can be changed) in the 6th Chakra depending on how you use your "mind's eye" to perceive your physical self, your qualities, and your characteristics. The choice is yours: You can see innumerable flaws or you can simply see perfection. This is also where creative visualization and the formation of one's life visions come into play.

Inspiration is the natural by-product of a balanced 6th Chakra, and people with open 6th Chakras live inspired and inspiring lives. They are wise, discerning, perceptive, and imaginative individuals who believe in themselves and their abilities, because ultimately they rely on their inner voice to show them the way. They look outside the box for solutions to challenges. A unique sense of personal style and individualism frequently throws the spotlight on them, their work, their homes, or their passions.

An overdeveloped 6th Chakra can be seen in "know-it-all" personality types. They are judgmental, inflexible, and pragmatic. They must see something in order to believe it, and they rarely, if ever, pay attention to or follow their feelings or inner guidance. Their closed minds most likely will prevent them from seeing the "bigger picture" of their lives.

People with an underdeveloped 6th Chakra may be fearful of change, of standing out, or of being in the limelight. They may suffer from aimlessness, unclear thinking, or lack of concentration. They may be prone to "follow the crowd" or to go along to get along, even when it is contrary to what they want or believe.

The Third Eye (or i i i) Formula for enlightenment is Imagination + Intuition + Insight = Inspired Action. Apply this method to your life and bask in the glow of "living in the light," then set your sights on the last level—the peak, the pinnacle of the Chakramid.

APPENDIX G
7th Chakra
(or Crown Chakra)

COLOR: Violet, White

ELEMENT: Thought

LOCATION: Top of the Head

AFFECTED PARTS OF BODY: Brain, Central Nervous System

MISSION STATEMENT: I Know

FOOD: None

CRYSTALS/GEMSTONES: Amethyst, Clear Quartz

SCENTS/ESSENTIAL OILS: Frankincense, Lavender, Lotus, Violet

The 7th Chakra, or Crown Chakra, is the last level in the Chakramid. Its shape naturally forms a pyramid inside the point of the Chakra Pyramid, and is itself made up of two levels. The lower, bottom half of the 7th Chakra level represents thoughts that are oriented toward the physical you—your health, your relationships, your wealth, your environment, and your possessions. Ultimately, these thoughts are deposited at the bottom, or base, of the Chakramid where they take root and bloom into physical manifestation. How fast (or how slow) thoughts manifest into physical reality depends largely upon how balanced or open the thinker's Chakras are. An open and direct passage through the Chakras allows thoughts to quickly come into being, while blockages and closures hamper, delay, or stop the physical manifesting process.

The second level of the 7th Chakra, up to the very tip of the Chakramid and beyond, symbolizes one's ascent to higher consciousness. This level transcends the physical and enters the realm of pure thought or pure consciousness. It is the seat of the One Mind or Infinite Intelligence.

People with balanced 7th Chakras are deeply connected with their spiritual sides. Their morals subtly drive their everyday actions. They are fair and ethical in their dealings with others. A reverence for life and nature is evident, and their wants and desires always seem to come easily and effortlessly to them.

An over-stimulated 7th Chakra can be seen in those who insist on being right no matter what, or may manifest in a "holier-than-thou" personality that is overwhelming and domineering. This narrow-mindedness or intolerance of others results in a closed mind that is incapable of expanding thought and consciousness.

People with deficient 7th Chakras may exhibit a neediness to be the center of attention or to make himself or herself indispensable. Conversely, they may become overly isolated or disconnected from others. "Going with the flow" in any situation is an impossibility because of an underlying belief that they (or their ego self) have to make things happen on their own. Constant worrying or obsessing over outcomes may plague such an individual.

The 7th Chakra has a dual nature—physical manifestation on one hand and the absence of anything physical on the other. It is multidimensional and ever expanding with thought and consciousness. At this last Chakra level, meditation is an indispensable tool for achieving higher consciousness, as is communion with nature. As you begin exploring your relationship with the 7th Chakra, know that it is not a destination, and that your journey in it will never end.

JOURNAL WITH JESSICA

Use the following pages to record your own Chakramid Reflections—your thoughts and the revelations you perceive about your Chakras as you read the story of Jessica's journey or after you have finished it.

CHAKRAMID JOURNAL
My 1st Chakra Reflections

CHAKRAMID JOURNAL
My 2nd Chakra Reflections

CHAKRAMID JOURNAL
My 3rd Chakra Reflections

CHAKRAMID JOURNAL
My 4th Chakra Reflections

CHAKRAMID JOURNAL
My 5th Chakra Reflections

CHAKRAMID JOURNAL
My 6th Chakra Reflections

CHAKRAMID JOURNAL
My 7th Chakra Reflections

www.Chakramid.com

Please visit our website, www.Chakramid.com, for resources that will help you learn more about balancing your Chakras.

You can also purchase our Chakramid™ Guided Journal, pen, gemstone jewelry and other inspirational items.